RAISE YOUR GAME

A STAND-ALONE NOVEL

CASSIA LEO

GLOSS PUBLISHING LLC

RAISE YOUR GAME
by Cassia Leo
cassialeo.com

ISBN-13: 978-1730986536

CHAPTER 1

LOGAN

*A*s I slide into the raven-haired CEO of Brunswick Publishing, I hear another squeak.

"Did you hear that? Do we have mice?" asks the muffled voice of a man, his question immediately followed by another squeak from my closet-companion.

I freeze mid-thrust. "*Shh*. We have to be quiet," I remind Helen Brunswick as I press her *too-thin-for-my-taste* body against the back wall of the coat closet, where we are currently celebrating our new partnership.

Helen just agreed to sell the majority share in her failing publishing company to my father's cutthroat investment firm, Angel Investments. We aren't really angel investors, and we're far from angels. My father, brother, and I are highly skilled in the art of hostile takeovers. Though, my technique is much less hostile.

What can I say? I'm a lover, not a fighter.

Helen giggles softly. "I'll be quiet as a mouse," the forty-three-year-old CEO says in a babyish voice.

Quiet as a mouse? Is this woman serious?

I shake my head as I thrust into her again. *Squeak.* Thrust. *Squeak.* Thrust. *Squeak.* Rolling my eyes, I realize I'm going to have to take a different approach with this squeaker toy before someone hears her and finds us in here.

No one can find us in here. I've been warned a million times by my father and the ethics committee at Angel Investments that I'm not allowed to use my cock to get women to sign on the dotted line. My father didn't think it was funny when I mentioned that, unlike my older brother Everett, *my* dick isn't pointy enough to sign anything.

Coiling my right arm around Helen's waist, I pull her flush against my chest and whisper in her ear, "Do you like it rough?"

"Oh, yes," she moans.

"How about we do a little roleplaying. I'm a dirty —but devastatingly handsome—pirate, and you're a ripe, beautiful maiden. I've come to have my way with you before I pillage your town."

The scenario wasn't very far from the truth, but Helen didn't seem to catch the symbolism.

She lets out a breathy chuckle. "You're so naughty, Logan. I love it. I'll be anything and anyone you want. Just don't stop fucking me."

I tighten my arm around her waist and gently clasp my other hand over her mouth as I whisper, "Aye, fair maiden. I'll be taking what I want," I say in an awful pirate accent, keeping one hand over her mouth as I slide my other hand between her thighs. "And what I want is your sweet, sweet nectar."

And by nectar, I'm referring to the majority stake in your $322 million publishing company.

I rub her swollen bud as she breathes heavily against the palm of my hand. Then, I thrust into her harder, my eight-inch cock slamming into her cervix. She takes this as a cue to begin acting the part of fair maiden—a little too enthusiastically.

This time she doesn't squeak. This time she screams. And her scream is so loud and high-pitched, I'll have tinnitus for a month.

"Shit!" I whisper as I frantically pull out of her and attempt to tuck my throbbing erection into my pants.

"I'm so sorry!" Helen whispers as she bends over to reach for the pink G-string wrapped around her ankles.

But the coat closet in the employee break room at Brunswick Publishing is too small, and she can't seem to bend over far enough. Every time she tries, she grinds her bare ass against the bulge in my pants.

"Hurry up! I hear voices coming," I urge.

"I can't reach my panties. You need to get out first!"

I reach for my zipper and pull it up, but it snags on my shirt tail. "Fuck!" I whisper as I try to unzip it, but it's stuck.

I try yanking the fabric to rip it out of the zipper, but it won't budge. Now, I'm not only standing in a closet with the bare-assed CEO, I'm also flushed and sweaty, with a waning erection in my pants.

I quickly button my pants and the top button on my suit jacket, but that's clearly not enough to cover up the indecency below my waist. The fashion police will have to forgive me this once as I button the second button on my jacket, which works only slightly better to cover up the bulge and the bunny-ear of white fabric sticking out of my zipper.

I don't hear any more voices outside the closet, so this is probably the right time to sneak out. But as I spin around and open the door, I get tangled in a red wool sweater. I try to pull it off me, but the metal hanger comes off the rod and hooks onto my collar, poking me in the back of the neck.

"Shit!" I whisper, contorting my body so I can reach back and remove the hanger from my collar. "Get it off me!"

"Get what off you? Hurry up!"

Somehow, the stupid sweater will not fall away. It's

sticking to my jacket like static cling. Finally, red-faced and feeling as if I'm about to combust with frustration, I throw open the closet door to escape the demon sweater. Standing in the middle of the employee break room is a group of at least a dozen people, all staring at me as I step out of the closet with a semi.

"That's one way to come out of the closet," says a male voice that sounds like it's coming from the back of the group.

Some of them snicker. Some of the women look crestfallen. A silver-haired man I recognize as the head of acquisitions is staring at me with his mouth agape. One group of three guys near the coffee machine seem to be paying each other—probably making good on a wager of how long it would take me to get into Helen's panties.

"What are you waiting for?" Helen whispers, clearly still facing the back of the closet. "Hurry up so I can get my underwear on."

I smile as I softly close the door behind me. "She thought she heard a mouse in there, so I was just trying to help her find it."

The three guys near the coffee machine chuckle as they continue settling their bets.

Helen emerges from the closet, her raven hair disheveled as she straightens her skirt. "This isn't what it looks like. Mr. Pierce was merely helping me…reach something up...high...in the... He's very tall. Very...big."

An older woman in an ivory pantsuit stares at my crotch and scrunches her nose in disgust. "Have you no shame?"

I cock an eyebrow as I flash the old woman my best seductive smile. "Wanna find out?"

***

"TO SAY I'm disappointed with you right now would be an understatement and completely useless," my father begins as he pours two glasses of bourbon from a crystal decanter in his corner office at Angel Investments. Keeping one drink for himself, he hands the other to my brother Everett. "It is blatantly clear you have no regard for how your actions reflect on the company, and you've once again left me with the task of cleaning up your mess."

"I can fix this," I say, pouring myself a drink.

"How?" my father demands, unbuttoning his jacket before taking a seat at his desk. "Helen has already been warned by her board of directors that any deal with our name on it will be rejected. And might I remind you, there are a plethora of investors eager to buy them out. Not to mention Ronald just informed me the ethics committee will be reviewing your work on this acquisition."

Everett takes a seat in the chair across from my father, leaning back with a smug grin on his face. "Yeah, how are you going to fix this, Logan? Going to offer to go down on old Helen this time?"

I chuckle at his barb. "For your information, brother, forty-year-old women are great in bed. They're just not very easy to bribe."

Everett rolls his eyes at my reference to the fact that the ethics committee has had to investigate—and cover up—at least four of his acquisitions for suspected bribery.

"All right. That's quite enough," my father interrupts, setting his tumbler of bourbon on the desk and expelling a heavy sigh. "You've *both* been caught with your pants down more times than I can count."

"I've never slept with a client," Everett insists.

"I was speaking metaphorically. I know you're more like your mother, Everett, about as subtle as a sledgehammer to the head, but do try to keep up."

I stifle a laugh. "With all due respect, Dad, I hardly think having sex is on par with bribery. One of those is clearly illegal."

My father narrows his eyes at me. "Some people might think sleeping with someone to get ahead in business is a form of prostitution."

"And those people have no understanding of the law," I reply.

My father shakes his head, probably regretting

that he forced me to get a law degree. "I've given you *both* more than enough chances to turn away from these unscrupulous tactics. It's time I do something about it. Something drastic."

"Cue the ultimatum," I remark, taking a seat in the chair next to Everett.

My father's distinguished air of discontent unravels into a devilish grin. "I think you'll like this ultimatum, son. In fact," he continues, shooting a glance in Everett's direction, "I think you'll both be very pleased. Provided you follow the rules, one of you stands to make spectacular gains."

Everett cocks an eyebrow. "Could we dispense with the cryptic allusions and discuss this ultimatum you speak of?"

My father chuckles. "Everett, I realize patience was never your strong suit. I understood this the moment you bribed a classmate to be your friend in primary school. You've never had the patience to cultivate relationships. You've always seen money as the only tool in your box."

I brace myself as my father turns to me. "Go ahead. Hit me with your best shot."

"You're also impatient, Logan," he continues. "You think your good looks are your key to success. Taking women straight to bed instead of courting them is your only approach. It's no surprise to me you're still single at your age."

I chuckle with disbelief. "I'm twenty-eight. I'm in my prime. There's nothing wrong with enjoying life before you settle down. If we're going to talk about singlehood reaching its expiration date, *you've* been divorced for seven years. When are *you* going to get back in the saddle, old boy?"

My father nods and smiles. "Funny you should mention that. I've met someone new, and I've decided to retire."

"What?" Everett blurts out.

"What Everett means is...what the hell, Dad?" I exclaim. "We haven't even met her and you're suddenly going to retire just so you can be with her? Are you two engaged? Is it... It is a woman, right?"

My father rolls his eyes. "Prissy is most definitely a woman. And not that it's any of your business, but, yes, we are engaged. As for you two meeting her, I've already scheduled a dinner for Sunday." He pauses to appreciate our slack-jawed expressions for a moment, then continues. "As for the ultimatum... Now that I'm retiring, I'll need one of you to take the majority share in the company, as I won't have much time for board meetings once Prissy and I are traveling."

Everett laughs, setting his tumbler on the desk and combing his fingers through his dark hair as he leans back in the chair. "I accept. Rest assured the company will be in good hands."

I roll my eyes. "A little quick on the draw there,

Everett. You might want to button the snap on the old bribery holster and let him finish. Besides, Father knows I'm clearly the better brother for the job."

"Better at *what*?" Everett bellows.

"Oh, I think we know what you're better at, Logan. All of New York knows what you're better at," my father continues, his nostrils flaring with exasperation. "As I was saying, I just struck a deal with Kensington Publishing. I have your uncle working on their fitness magazine division, but I want you to work on putting together a business revitalization plan for their nature magazine, *Open Sky*," he says to Everett. "And you, Logan, will be making a plan for their celebrity gossip magazine, *Close-Up*."

"You've got to be kidding me. That rag has dumped on me for years, and now I'm supposed to save them from bankruptcy?" I protest, my voice jumping at least two octaves like a child protesting chores.

Close-Up magazine used to be the most popular celebrity gossip rag on the shelf, until some antiquated marketing tactics and bad management failed to deliver them into the digital age. Now they've apparently sold out to my father in a last ditch effort to save themselves from bankruptcy. That means it's our responsibility to do what their upper management should have done years ago and hope it's not too late.

Our company doesn't usually buy out another company with the intention of revamping them. Sure, we will usually pitch that as a good possibility. But most of the time, we break up the company, lay off scores of employees to cut costs, and liquidate all assets before moving on.

But trying to save a company is no small feat. And trying to save a celebrity lifestyle magazine like *Close-Up*... Well, let's just say this is not my father's usual modus operandi. This Prissy woman must be making him soft.

"I'm aware both of these companies will present many obstacles for you two. But I'm certain you'll rise to the challenge. Whoever's plan has the most positive effect on the bottom line at the end of thirty days will be awarded the majority share in Angel Investments."

"Thirty days?" Everett exclaims. "Surely, you must be joking. We can't do this in thirty days."

My father drains the rest of the bourbon in his glass then leans back in his tufted mahogany leather chair. "I have faith in you both. Just keep your bribes to yourself, Everett. And you," he says, glaring at me. "Keep your hands to yourself. Don't let me down."

———

I ENTER my office and immediately make a call to

beckon my assistant Nora. "Close the door," I say as soon as she arrives.

She shuts the door softly and turns to face me, her auburn hair framing her eager face as she holds her mobile phone behind her back. "What can I help you with, sir?"

Nora is a great assistant. She wears her hair down to hide the custom-fitted Bluetooth earpiece-slash-microphone in her ear. It records every command I give her, so she can replay our conversations in the event she forgets what she was told to do. I don't want this conversation recorded.

I tap my ear and say, "Give it to me."

She doesn't hesitate as she removes the gel earpiece and places it on my desk in front of me.

"And the phone."

She places her iPhone next to it.

I quickly snatch it up and power off the phone before I begin. "I have a special project for you, but no one can know about this. Do you understand?"

She mimes pulling a zipper across her lips. "My lips are sealed."

"Good," I say, motioning to the chair across from me. "Have a seat."

CHAPTER 2

The entire editorial department, all twenty-one of us spread out across thirty-two cubicles, are silent as ghosts. As we pretend to make phone calls and chase down salacious leads, we steal occasional glances in the direction of the glass walls surrounding the conference room. Inside the room, seated in a steel mesh chair at a long table, is my best friend Jennifer Christoff, assistant to the editor-in-chief at *Close-Up* magazine. Seated across from Jen is our editor-in-chief, my former fling and new worst enemy, Brady Harper.

Brady has let go six of our coworkers in the editorial department over the past three months. Jen will be the first coworker to bite the dust who isn't an unscrupulous, entitled little snowflake. Unfortunately, the fact that she's Brady's assistant and not a piece of shit does not bode well for the rest of us.

I know Brady's only following orders from the higher-ups — cost-cutting measures in a waning print magazine market. I sometimes consider writing an anonymous op-ed about the time he cried when we had sex. But I could never do that, especially since Brady did save my father and me from near-homelessness two years ago.

My worst fears are confirmed as Jen exits the conference room looking like her beloved miniature poodle Knickknack has just passed away. Her dark-brown hair obscures her round face as she walks with her head hung low, presumably in a daze. The usual sway in her curvy hips is gone.

I sigh as I realize I'll be next.

If Brady laid off his own assistant, who's been at *Close-Up* longer than I have, my head is *definitely* on the chopping block. An editorial assistant like me, who's already on probation… I might as well just hand them the executioner's axe. Actually, except for my ability to get almost anyone to dish gossip on any celebrity, I'm not sure why I'm still here.

For the past two years, Brady and I have had to attend a probation review hearing every six months, where we're called into a meeting with the director of human resources, Jane Rowell. Jane assesses whether Brady and I have been pulling our weight, making sure we're violating as few privacy laws as possible while still getting the good celebrity scoops. Also, she likes to check that I haven't been taking too many days off or taking two-hour-long dumps in the employee restroom.

Oh, and whether I've finished paying off the insanely high-interest personal loan issued to me by *Close-Up* magazine two years ago.

At the time, I was in desperate need of money to pay my father's past due mortgage, which he'd fallen behind on because he drained his bank accounts to pay for a special wheelchair. Brady, being privy to aspects of my personal life, suggested a $47,000 advance on my salary. Brady authorized the personal loan, which is only *part* of the reason we're both on probation.

The other reason being the six-week fling Brady and I engaged in shortly before I was promoted from copy editor to editorial assistant. Despite the fact our fling was very much over when I received the promotion, and Brady was dating someone new by the time I received the personal loan, Jane Rowell insisted our previous connection made the promotion and loan seem like a quid-pro-quo.

As if I'd ever sleep with someone for a raise.

As Jen takes a seat in the empty cubicle next to mine instead of her own desk, she stares at the blank computer screen for a while in a daze. I give her a moment to process whatever happened in the conference room, then I stand from my chair and go to her, wrapping my arms around her soft shoulders.

We are quickly joined by our thirty-seven-year-old coworker Gail Henderson. She's ten years our senior, but Gail is every bit one of the girls. And Jen will need Gail's words of wisdom today.

"Look on the bright side," I say, trying to maintain cheery tone. "Now you won't have to take Knickknack to that expensive doggy day care."

"But he loves doggy day care," she pouts. "What if I never find another job and I have to live with my parents for the rest of my life?"

"You'll find another job in no time," Gail replies fiercely. "You're great at what you do."

Jen sighs. "Not as great as you two," she replies, looking at me. "Miss Celebrity Whisperer."

I tuck my curly light-brown hair behind my ear, almost blushing at the mention of my nickname around the office. "Believe me, being able to convince a disgruntled chauffeur or personal assistant to dish on a celebrity is not going to save me from the unemployment line. I read an article just last week about how some of the biggest publishing houses in New York are being bought out by investors. They're cutting staff left and right. My days are numbered."

Jen narrows her eyes at me. "You read this last week and you didn't think it was important enough to share with me? Now, I'm going to have to start buying the cheap dog food and Knickknack is going to die."

Her question jolts me into defense. "Well, I didn't think you'd be let go. You're too important to Brady. You're too important to *Close-Up*."

Jen's face softens as she lets out a deep sigh. "It doesn't matter. I should have seen it coming. Normally, Brady will ask me to go down to HR and pick up an employee audit report. I opened the folder and peeked at the report a couple of times, and I figured out Brady uses it to see who has the most negative points against them."

"Negative points?" I say as Gail and I exchange a confused look.

Jen shakes her head. "Negative points are things like unplanned absences, no degree, disciplinary actions, and, get this, a high salary."

Gail and I gasp.

"That dirty little weasel," Gail snarls.

Jen nods as she continues. "Well, whoever has the most negative points and the highest salary ends up canned within two days of Brady asking for the report." She pauses a moment to look around, presumably to make sure no one is eavesdropping on our conversation. "Anyway, two weeks ago, he asked me to get the report again. When I peeked inside, I noticed that *I* was now the highest paid employee with the most negative points."

My eyes widen. "Because of your vacation to brown town?" I ask, referring to when Jen ate some bad Indian food and got explosive diarrhea a few months ago. She was out sick for six days, two of which she was hospitalized for severe dehydration.

"Diarrhea kills more than two million people every year!" Gail proclaims.

Technically, Jen's illness wasn't planned, so it *did* result in an unplanned absence, but it wasn't exactly her fault.

Jen shrugs. "I literally flushed my career down the toilet."

"Wait a minute," I say, holding up a finger. "You said he got the report two weeks ago, but normally it only takes him two days to let someone go. What went wrong?"

She purses her lips and shrugs. "He claims he was fighting for me to stay, but he was overruled. I don't know if I believe him, but I guess it doesn't really matter. Either way, I'm still out of a job."

I shake my head in disbelief. "You'll find another job. There are plenty of editorial positions on ZipRecruiter. Or you can freelance."

"Yeah, I'm not sure I want to stay in a business where people think it's okay to stalk celebrities and go through their trash cans to find out if they've cheated on their paleo diet," Jen says.

Gail crosses her thin arms across her chest and

leans against the cubicle partition as she lets out a hoarse cackle. "No kidding. We should all be looking for jobs now."

I shake my head. "I'm not sure why I'm still here, with my being on probation and all. I'm sure I'll be joining you very soon."

Jen shakes her head. "Doubt it. Your name never came up on those audit reports."

"What?" I say, unable to hide my shock. "That doesn't even make sense. I must have the most negative points of anyone at this company. I mean, I have so many negative points, I'm practically the Knicks."

Jen looks up at me, her brown eyes shimmering with a glint of hope. "You should apply for that new opening at *Open Sky* for travel features editor," she replies.

I shake my head adamantly. "No, I am not applying for *any* positions within Kensington Publishing. If they're downsizing *Close-Up*, they're probably laying off people at *Open Sky*, too. Besides, I'm not qualified to be an editor."

"You are *beyond* qualified," Jen replies.

I smile at Jen's ferocity. It *does* take a bit of nuance to be good at this job.

Most gossip columnists are just looking for a steady paycheck. It's usually the editors who are to blame for the sensationalized stories and headlines. Most columnists don't actually believe half the crap they write. Of course, that only makes it all the more repulsive. Sensationalism sells, so editors package it to have the most punch.

The truth is, what you see published in gossip columns and tabloid rags is far less sensational than what some of these editors *want* to print.

And most of these so-called "journalists" have very poor opinions of their readers. I once heard Rita Brenner, the editorial assistant in our celebrity style section, say that our target audience is "idiots, fascists, and self-loathing stay-at-home moms." That soulless bloodsucker was promoted to managing style editor a few months later.

It's true. Many gossip columnists — though not all — are as awful as we imagine they are. But there are still plenty of decent ones out there. I'd like to think I'm one of the good ones.

"You know what we need?" Jen declares. "We need midnight margaritas."

I cock an eyebrow. "Is that a *Practical Magic* reference?"

Jen smiles. "Margaritas and a Sandra Bullock marathon cures everything!"

Gail shakes her head. "I have swim practice with the kiddo tonight. You guys will have to do midnight margaritas without me," she says, patting Jen on the back. "I'll bake you some of your favorite cream-filled, penis-shaped Twinkies."

Jen's face lights up like a kid on Christmas. "I want chocolate filling this time."

I rub her arm. "Of course you do."

FOUR MARGARITAS and two Sandra Bullock movies down, and Jen and I are sloshed. She plops down onto the sofa next to me, spilling a little bit of the lime margarita in her hand onto my bare thigh. I gasp as she positions herself next to me while trying to wipe away the sticky liquid from my skin with the cuff of her cream cashmere cardigan.

"You're going to ruin your sweater," I proclaim, pushing her hand away.

Jen holds up her damp sleeve. "This is cashmere. Do you know how cashmere is made?"

I chuckle. "What?"

"It's made from a goat. Goats are ruminants."

I blink a few times as I try to bring Jen's face into focus. "I think you should stop moving or I'm going to spew the ruminants of my last margarita all over you."

We stare at each other for a moment before we burst into uncontrollable laughter. When she's composed herself, she takes one more sip and sets her drink on my coffee table. Scooping up my laptop, she places it on her thighs and begins navigating to the company website login. Using my credentials, she logs in and quickly finds the page soliciting applications for a travel features editor for *Open Sky* magazine. In my inebriated state, I make zero protest as she uploads my resume and enters all the necessary information.

She clicks 'Submit' and raises her arms in the air like an Olympic gymnast who's just nailed a difficult dismount. "Done!" she declares with pride. "What do we watch next? *The Proposal?*"

I nod fervently. "Oh, yeah. Give me some of that sweet Ryan Reynolds man-chest."

But as Jen is about to close the lid on my laptop, the ding of a new email gets our attention.

"It's probably just a confirmation that your application was received," she says, closing the lid.

I smile as I snatch the laptop from her and slur, "You never know. It could be Brady responding. 'Sophie, you can't work at *Open Sky*. I can't lose you. I'll double your salary if you stay.'"

"Or maybe it's Ryan Reynolds," Jen replies deadpan, staring at me in silence for a long moment before we both burst into laughter again. "Hurry up and check it while I get the movie ready."

I open my laptop and click on the Gmail tab in my browser. The subject of the email reads: Re: New Application for Travel Features Editor. The name of the person it's from reads: Interim AI. Must be some sort of artificial intelligence responder system. I click the subject line to open the email.

Dear Mrs. Bishop:

I regret to inform you that *Open Sky* magazine and *Close-Up* magazine have been bought out. Therefore, we are now in the midst of a hiring and promotion freeze as we attempt to reorganize. Talented as you may be, in theory or reality, your application for travel features editor is hereby denied.

Have a wonderful weekend.

Respectfully,

Mr. Pierce, Interim CEO of *Close-Up* magazine

"Bought out?" Jen says, staring at my screen.

"In theory or reality?" I say in utter shock.

"No wonder they've been laying people off left and right," Jen continues. "They're trying to make

Kensington look more attractive to investors. Such *bullshit*."

I stare at her, mouth agape. "Is that all you took away from that email? Did you not see how rude this asshole is? I mean, what kind of scum uses the phrase 'Talented as you may be, in theory or reality'?"

Jen shakes her head as she grabs her margarita off the coffee table and sits back again. "It's not like you can do anything about it. What are you going to do? Demand an apology?"

My nostrils flare as I realize the injustice of it, then I begin typing a response as Jen looks on. She gives me suggestions for better insults, and we laugh hysterically as we go back and forth composing the perfect reply email, which I will obviously never send. But it's nice to *pretend* we have spines.

I sit back and chuckle as I read the email one last time before I delete it.

Dear Mr. Pierce:

For your information, my name is *Ms*. Bishop, not Mrs. The last time I checked, there is no wedding ring on my *talented* finger. In fact, my fingers are *so* talented, they're probably better suited to flipping you off than typing up blathering gossip about B-list celebrities. You can take your promotion and shove it up your tight, shriveled asshole.

I *will* have a wonderful weekend, using my talented fingers to look for another job, while you use yours to jerk yourself off.

Respectfully,

Sophie Bishop, Staff Writer/Editorial Assistant and Certified Badass

---

JEN *TSKS* as she grabs the laptop. "Okay, enough admiring our work. It's time to watch —"

My life flashes before my eyes as Jen loses her grip on her drink and it begins to tip toward my computer. Without hesitation, I snatch the laptop away, one hand clumsily covering the keyboard as my other reaches underneath to stop it from falling. Jen's drink spills on my arm, but only a tiny splash hits the keyboard. I quickly use my shirt sleeve to wipe the liquid away, then I hold the laptop upside down, with the keyboard facing the floor to let gravity do the rest of the work.

"I'm so sorry!" Jen cries.

I laugh as I wipe the keyboard a bit more before

turning it right side up again. "It's no big deal. It's a laptop. If it's ruined, I can get another one."

But my easy-going demeanor is quickly erased when I look at the screen. In the process of trying to wipe away the liquid, I accidentally sent the email.

Suddenly, I'm very sober.

I WALK into the ground floor lobby of Kensington Publishing, and I'm immediately accosted by Gail. Her thin blonde hair seems to be only halfway blown out, and she only has makeup on one eye.

"What happened to you? You look like your house caught on fire while you were getting ready this morning," I say as she attempts to block my path toward the elevator. "What are you doing?"

Her blue eyes are wide with fright. "Jen called me this morning to tell me what happened this weekend… at your little Sandra Bullock movie marathon party."

"Oh, yeah. It was such a blast. I'm sorry you couldn't be there."

Gail waves off my apology. "Never mind that. I'm talking about the email heard 'round the world."

I roll my eyes. "I know. It was horrible, but it's not as if I'm not going to be fired already. I just have to suck it up, go up there, and take it like a woman."

Gail shakes her head adamantly. "No, no, no. You

don't understand." She fixes me with a grave expression. "I got a call from Harold yesterday morning. He said Brady was let go after we left the office on Friday. The new editor-in-chief and interim CEO of *Close-Up* magazine is Jasper Pierce."

I shrug. "I know. He signed the email he sent me and I Googled him. I'm familiar with his son, I think his name is Logan. Typical man-whore with a trust fund. But I don't know much about Jasper, other than he seems to favor hostile takeovers."

Gail shakes my shoulders a bit, possibly to shake me out of my complacency. "He's up there right now."

I stare at her for a moment as I try to decide if I should panic. "It's not as if I didn't expect this. Though, admittedly, I didn't expect to be ambushed first thing in the morning."

"Well, you never know," she says, her panicked tone evolving into a maniacal faux optimism. "Maybe your reply email didn't even go through. Maybe that's why he never responded."

I chuckle. "Yeah, and maybe he's decided to forgive my $30,000 loan balance and give me a raise. Wee!"

Her shoulders slump as she realizes there is no use trying to sugarcoat this. I'm getting canned today.

"Okay, so what's the plan," I ask.

Gail narrows her eyes at me as she thinks. "Maybe you should consider groveling?"

I let out a deep sigh. "Why do I mess everything up?"

Gail's expression hardens. "You do *not* mess everything up! You're a smart, caring, capable young woman. And anyone in your situation," she continues, alluding to the two and a half years I took care of my father in the latter stages of his illness. "would have been hustling to make ends meet. You did nothing wrong."

"Thanks for the pep talk. So what am I going to do?"

Gail straightens her back and pulls back her shoulders. "You are going to march in there and apologize for the unfortunate email mishap. Then, you're going to demand an apology, because no one — not even Jasper Pierce — gets to talk to you like you're some kind of loser."

I chuckle softly. "I think that may be the worst advice you've ever given me."

She purses her lips at me. "Hey, I didn't get to where I am today by letting assholes like Jasper Pierce walk all over me."

I scrunch my eyebrows in confusion. "But...you haven't had a raise in almost two years."

"Oh, right. Well, so much for my pep talk. We have to go up before we're late."

Gail locks elbows with me and pulls me toward the elevator. With a determined expression on her face, she punches the button for the sixteenth floor and unlocks her arm from mine as we stand side-by-side in the elevator cab.

The tension is as thick and menacing as cobwebs. Gail has always been assertive, maybe even a bit pushy and motherly, which I've always welcomed since my own mother died when I was seventeen. But the sober, determined expression on her face is making me a bit nervous. My paranoia assumes she may know more about my fate with *Close-Up* than she's letting on, but the reality is probably that she knows more about what it's like to get laid off.

She and her husband both lost their jobs during the recession. She used to be an editor at now-defunct *Gourmet* magazine, before they ceased publication and their brand was moved to epicurious.com. Her husband was a foreman for a government contractor. It took almost six years for them to start earning as much as they were before the recession. They downsized everything in the process. Their plan to have three kids was scrapped as they agreed to focus all their love — and finances — on the one they already had.

At the twelfth floor, the elevator stops and picks up another occupant, a woman in a peach cardigan and gray slacks, whom I recognize as Laura Bernard from the circulation department.

Laura flashes me a tight smile. "We're all going up," she proclaims, sounding much too chipper.

My eyebrows shoot up for a second, then I smile back. "Yep, that's where I work."

At least, that's where I work for now.

A painful expression spreads across Laura's demure features. "You don't think this has to do with the personal time I had to take last year?" she asks. "I mean, I had to take a lot of time off when my husband was on *The Voice*. He made it all the way to week three!"

It seems the paranoia surrounding the lack of job stability at *Close-Up* has seeped into every department and every floor of this company. I feel bad for Laura. I do. But I can't let her fear trickle into my psyche like toxic sludge.

So I do what any decent coworker would do in this situation.

I smile as I wave off her concern. "I'm sure you have nothing to worry about. I've heard we have a new interim CEO. Maybe they're calling you up to give you a raise."

Gail flashes me an *are-you-crazy* sort of look. A knot of guilt twists inside my belly as I realize I *am* grateful it was Laura who was called to the editor-in-chief's office this morning instead of me. Not that I can't still be called to his office, but I must celebrate these small victories while I still can.

As we exit the elevator on the sixteenth floor, Laura heads to the left and Gail and I turn right, in the direction of our cubicles. Just as I begin to entertain the possibility that I might not actually be fired today, I arrive at my cubicle to find a Post-It note on my iMac screen. The note reads:

SEE me in my office at 9:35 sharp.
   -Chief

IT DOESN'T LOOK like Brady's handwritten. And Brady only signs his notes "Chief" or "Editor-in-Chief" when he's addressing someone other than me. Of course, this practice only served to fuel the rumors that Brady and I were still in item, despite the fact that Brady has been dating a supermodel for almost a year. The brief, almost curt tone in this note, the handwriting I don't recognize, and the rumors that Brady has been let go, tell me this message was probably written by Jasper Pierce.

Taking my phone out of my purse, I glance at the time on the screen: 9:04. I have thirty-one minutes to formulate an excuse for why I sent that email to our interim CEO.

Gail heads to her cubicle, which is about four cubes away from mine. Leaving her giant handbag on her desk, she returns to stand behind me as we both stare at the Post-It note in my hand.

"Well, you have half an hour to practice your groveling face," she begins, a note of optimism in her voice. "Okay, jot this down."

I take a seat in my desk chair and stick the note in the upper right-hand corner of my screen. Turning on my computer, I tap my fingers on the desk impatiently as it goes through the loading screen and my desktop finally materializes before us. Opening up the TextEdit application, I begin typing an apology email as dictated to me by Gail.

Dear Sir,

I am very much humbled to write to you asking forgiveness for my highly inappropriate email. I know there is no excuse for the type of rude and crude language I used, especially in a professional setting.

I have been under enormous stress lately due to rumors around the office of inevitable dismissals and layoffs, as well as my own financial hardships, of which you are probably well aware. Furthermore, I understand I am solely responsible for this temporary lapse in judgment, and I take full responsibility for any consequences resulting from my inappropriate behavior.

Though I understand that my actions may be unforgivable, I want to reiterate my sincerest apology to you and the entire editorial team, whom I may have embarrassed with my actions. I sincerely assure you that no such lapse in judgment will ever happen again as long as I am employed by Kensington Publishing.

Yours truly,

Sophie Bishop, Staff Writer/Editorial Assistant

I STARE at the letter for a moment, wondering if maybe I should just save the apology for the 9:35 a.m. meeting with Jasper. Though the possibility of completely avoiding a confrontation with him by sending an email is very tempting, I feel he will be much more likely to accept my apology if I deliver it in person.

I close the program without copying the text or saving the document.

Gail lets out a soft gasp. "What are you doing? You have to copy the text into an email."

I shake my head. "No, I'm not going to send that in an email. I need to apologize in person. Besides, do I really want to defend myself via the same method in which I committed my crime? That would be like showing up graveside wearing nothing but pasties to a funeral for a man who died of a heart attack in a strip club. That doesn't seem very smart."

Gail's eyes widen. "You're equating a meeting with your boss to a funeral?"

I let out a deep sigh. "Oh, God. I'm *so* fired."

Gail gives my shoulders a squeeze. "Well, if Miss Celebrity Whisperer is fired, I can't be far behind you. I'll be at my desk if you need me, sweetheart."

I try to keep myself busy for half an hour, checking email and browsing popular posts on rival mags, but it does nothing to calm my nerves. At a few minutes to 9:35 a.m., I pop up from my chair and make my way toward the editor-in-chief's office. As I pass by Jen's old desk, which now stands empty, my anxiety ratchets up a notch. When I arrive at the maple door, with Brady's nameplate on it, I knock softly.

A deep voice calls out from within. "Come on in!"

My curiosity is piqued as I know Jasper Pierce is in his sixties, but the voice I just heard sounded much younger. Maybe somebody is in there with him? I reach for the steel door handle and turn it slowly, pushing the door inward as I slip inside. The man sitting at Brady's old desk is definitely *not* Jasper Pierce or Brady.

Like Brady, this man has dark hair, but his is a tad longer on top, and much more stylish. Even sitting in Brady's chair, I can tell this guy is much taller than Brady's five-foot–eleven–inch frame. Nor does he have the soft, kind lines of Brady's thirty-four-year-old face.

This man's face is all angles: strong jaw, chiseled cheekbones, symmetrical Patrician nose. And he doesn't have Brady's green eyes. This man's eyes are an icy steel-gray that penetrates me as his gaze rakes over my body, from the top of my head down to the toes of my black pumps. And that's all I need to confirm that he is indeed who I think he is: Logan Pierce.

Logan Pierce looks as polished and cool as he does in every paparazzi photo I've ever seen, but his eyes are different in person. They're focused on mine like a missile. The intense look hints at the man behind the steel-gray eyes, a man coiled too tightly, a snake ready strike.

He leans back in Brady's chair and smiles, looking very pleased. "You're Sophie Bishop?"

I don't answer his question right away. This is partly because I'm a bit stunned by this new and unexpected turn of events. But also because I might actually have a chance at digging myself out of the hole I dug with my "email heard 'round the world."

Logan Pierce is a notorious playboy in the Manhattan social scene. He's probably bedded more celebrities than I've written about in my entire six-year career at *Close-Up*. But he's smarter than the usual celebrity whore, because Logan doesn't stick around long enough to make headlines. He gets in and out, moving onto a new model or actress or heiress, before the ink has even dried.

I clear my throat as I straighten my spine and pull my shoulders back, just as Gail did a few minutes ago. "Yes, I'm Sophie Bishop."

"Have a seat, Sophie," he says, motioning to a chair across from him.

I draw in a deep breath and try to relax as I take a seat across from one of New York City's most ruthless businessmen and most notorious womanizers. How do I even begin to formulate a plan for this meeting? While this may be a fortuitous turn of events, it's only an opportunity if I play my cards right.

"Do you know who I am, Sophie?" he asks, a note of mischief in his voice, almost as if he's daring me to pretend I don't know who he is.

"Yes, I know you are," I reply, keeping an even tone. "You're Logan Pierce. I assume it was you who responded to my application for the managing editor position at *Open Sky*?"

He nods. "Your assumption is correct," he replies proudly. "Do you know why I asked you in here this morning?"

I draw in another deep breath, stalling for time as I try to decide whether I should spew the apology Gail dictated to me a few minutes ago. But the longer I look at Logan's smirk, the less I want to apologize. After all, if he is the one who replied to me, *he* was the one who was rude to me first.

Talented as you may be, in theory or reality...

"I presume I'm here to be let go," I respond, keeping my tone professional and authoritative. "I'd appreciate if you could get it over with so I can gather my things and get on with my day."

Logan let's out a deep chuckle that's as rich and sexy as he is. "No, Sophie. You don't mind if I call you Sophie, do you?" He nods when I shake my head, indicating I don't mind. "Good. I think it's important that you and I get off on the right foot. You may call me Logan." He's silent for a moment, possibly waiting for me to respond, but when I don't he continues undaunted. "You're here today, Sophie, because I have a proposal for you."

I narrow my eyes at him. "What kind of proposal?" I ask, crossing my arms over my breasts.

He picks up on my body language quickly. "Not that kind of proposal. Well, actually, it is sort of like that, but... Actually, let me start this over."

He rises from the chair and plucks something off his desk that looks like a brochure. Rounding the desk, he sits down on the front edge, just a couple feet away from me, so now I have to tilt my face up to look him in the eye. If I didn't know better, I would think this is a power pose, his way of trying to assert physical dominance over me.

I'm not falling for this.

He hands me the brochure. "What do you think of that?"

I stare at the brochure for a moment, uncertain what type of reaction he is trying to get out of me. The brochure is clearly some type of promotional material for a couples retreat. But this is not just *any* couples retreat. This retreat is for married couples who are seeking to revive their sex lives with tantric intimacy.

I hand the brochure back to him. "Am I supposed to know what this means?"

He looks somewhat confused by my answer. "I was told you're the best person in the editorial department when it comes to securing celebrity exclusives. Is that not true?"

I uncross my arms and lean back in my chair a bit, wanting to appear more relaxed and confident. "Yes, I have been told I have a certain...way with celebrities."

Logan's face beams with curiosity as he stands up to head back and take a seat in Brady's chair again. "Okay, in case you haven't caught on yet, Brady

Harper no longer works at *Close-Up* magazine," he begins, his tone not at all conciliatory. "And, as I'm sure you are aware, his assistant no longer works here, as well. So I've been asked, as interim CEO, to take over Brady's editor-in-chief responsibilities. My first order of business is to hire a new assistant. Starting today, you will assume that role."

This time *I* let out a hearty chuckle. "Thank you, but I am really not cut out for administrative work. As you just mentioned, I am much better at my job in the gossip section."

Logan smiles and the sight of it makes my skin tingle. "Sophie, this is not a promotion that you can reject. You can take the position as my assistant or you can take your things and leave."

"Well, I think I would rather take my things and leave," I reply, bracing my hands on the arms of the chair as I prepare to get up and walk out. "Thank you very much for the opportunity. I'm sure someone else in the office would be happy to fill the position of your assistant."

I rise from the chair, but when I'm halfway to the door he begins to speak again.

"You might want to rethink that," he says. "You still owe Kensington Publishing $29,000 and some change. And since I just bought Kensington Publishing, that means you owe me that money. And if you leave now, I can file a civil claim. I can sue you and put a lien on any assets of value, whether that's a car or a house."

I stand facing the door as I attempt to collect myself. Anger brews inside me as I realize he's done his research. He knows why I had to borrow the money from Kensington Publishing. He knows the only thing I own in this world is the home my father willed to me after his death. And if he can put a lien on my property, I'll probably lose my childhood home. The home that both my mother and father died in.

I spin around with a smile on my face. "Okay, let's say I do take the position as your assistant," I begin as I make my way back to the chair I just vacated. "What does that have to do with a couples retreat?"

"You mean to tell me Miss Celebrity Whisperer doesn't already know?"

I fix Logan with a steely gaze. "How about we cut the crap? I know you got the scathing email I accidentally sent to you. And I know you know I've written some very critical articles about you. So why don't you just stop being cryptic and tell me what the brochure means, okay?"

He laughs again. "You could put the salt industry out of business with that mouth. Good God." He looks me up and down again before he continues. "Well, I'm sure you're aware that the famous celebrity couple comprised of Kitty Hawthorne and Jason Costello, more commonly referred to as Kitson or Jitty, have been having some marital problems as of late. Jason has been accused of getting a little too friendly with other as-of-yet unknown women. Kitty has been accused of denying him sex."

I roll my eyes. "Hold on. Let me find my shocked face... So typical. A man cheats and it must be the woman's fault."

Logan smiles as he continues. "Well, Kitty has a reputation as being a bit of a prima donna. But that's not what I brought you in here to discuss. I brought you in here because Kitty and Jason are rumored to be arriving at this resort, this couples retreat, in Honolulu this coming Friday. As I'm sure you're aware, all the celebrity news rags and tabloids are vying for the scoop on these two. Readers are dying to know if he cheated and with whom. This is where you come in."

"So you want me to go to this couples retreat and attempt to get an exclusive interview with Kitty Hawthorne and Jason Costello? Or do you want me to contact some of my sources and see if we can get an anonymous exclusive?"

He shrugs. "Well, first of all, I think it would be a bit difficult for a *single* woman to go to a *couples* retreat," he remarks, fixing me with a look that makes me feel naked. "Do you understand what I'm getting at, Sophie?"

I shake my head. "Are you suggesting...I have to

take someone with me on this retreat? But you said it yourself? I'm single. I don't have a boyfriend, much less a husband. What am I supposed to do? Ask someone to pretend to be my husband?" I remark with a chortle.

He nods. "That took you far longer to figure out than I expected it would, but yes, that is what I am implying."

Jerk.

I roll my eyes. "Who am I supposed to take with me?"

He looks me up and down again for the third time, his gaze lingering on my chest for just a millisecond longer than everywhere else. "Well, I know that you had somewhat of a history with the old editor-in-chief, Brady Harper. Though I wouldn't expect him to be your type, if I'm being honest."

My eyes widen with shock. "Excuse me? How would you know my type?"

A slow smile spreads across his godlike features. "I have a knack for these things." He pauses to relish the appalled expression on my face. "You and I will be going to the retreat together."

I cock an eyebrow. "Surely, you must be joking. Everyone in New York knows you're single. Very single."

"Not everyone. When was the last time you saw me in the papers?" he asks, waiting a moment until he's sure I'm not going to reply. "You see, I've been keeping a low profile for the past few weeks, and that is so I can pretend I got married recently."

I look him directly in the eye. "You want to pretend like you just got married within the last few weeks and you're *already* having problems in your sex life?"

He shakes his head. "I know it's a tough sell for someone like me, but there's no reason why we can't claim we've been married longer. Maybe we got married last year, spur of the moment wedding in Vegas. And my philandering has caused a rift between us."

"You want me to pretend that I married you and allowed you to have sex with whoever you wanted for the entire first year of our marriage?"

He's silent for a moment, studying my skeptical face. "Kitty Hawthorne and Jason Costello are not exactly the brightest bulbs. And I have full confidence in your ability to get the scoop on them. But if you doubt your ability, you are free to walk out that door and out of this building forever. Your choice."

I think about his words, rolling them over in my mind, flipping them, turning them around, trying to figure out how I can possibly use them against him. Has he violated any labor laws with this meeting? Probably not, considering he has every right to let me go. And the company has every right to collect the money I owe them. But the way he is framing this proposal does seem a bit like extortion or bribery.

Either way, I can't afford to hire a lawyer to fight Kensington Publishing or Logan's investment firm.

He looks me over again, his eyes lingering on my hair this time. "If you do this, you should dye your hair blonde to hide your identity. Actually...on second thought, maybe I should just get you a stylist."

I glare at him. "What are you trying to say?"

His eyes widen. "I didn't mean it as an insult. I just mean that you'll want to look as different as possible, so no one recognizes you."

"I'll skip the stylist, thanks."

"Like I said, your choice," he says with a shrug. "So what *is* your choice, Miss Celebrity Whisperer?"

I heave a deep sigh. "How long is this retreat?"

JEN'S WINE glasses have already been packed away, so Gail pours pinot grigio into our coffee mugs and takes a seat at the bar-height dining table in Jen's one-bedroom apartment in Chelsea. Moving boxes litter the modernly decorated space in various stages, some lie flat and unassembled, some gaping open and half-filled with her belongings, others taped shut and labeled in fat black marker.

Jen was laid off less than five days ago, and she's

already packing up to move in with her parents in Westchester, so she can start freelancing. She wants to be in control of her fate, despite the fact that the very nature of fate is its refusal to be controlled.

Gail places a chocolate-crème-filled homemade Twinkie in front of each of us. "You can't seriously be thinking of doing this," she says as she passes out napkins.

"Why not?" Jen shoots back, picking up her Twinkie. "It's a week in paradise with Mr. Gorgeous. And she gets a promotion and a raise. You *will* be getting a raise, right?"

"Of course," I reply, though the specifics of the raise are still unknown to me, as Logan promised to have his attorney write up an agreement, which I haven't seen yet.

"See?" Jen goads Gail. "She's getting paid. I don't know about you, but I'd *pay anything* for Logan Pierce to…treat me with respect."

Gail nods. "Well, if the rumors about Logan are true, he is *very* good at treating women with respect."

We all take a bite of our Twinkies and Jen's eyes roll back in her head. They really are way better than the original. Gail is a magician when it comes to baked goods.

I put my Twinkie down and wipe my fingers before reaching for my mug of wine. "Okay, can we please stop speculating on how good he is in bed and focus on how this could ruin my reputation," I remind Jen. "Journalistic integrity aside, do I really want to be the type of person who would marry a known womanizer? For a raise? Even if it is a fake marriage, doesn't that make me look weak or, God forbid, like some kind of gold-digger?"

Gail nods again. "You're right. This is a big decision. You have to consider this from all angles. For instance, if Kensington Publishing still goes under, will this affect your future job prospects?"

Jen rolls her eyes. "If anything, this will boost her future job prospects. With all his business contacts, I'm sure a stellar recommendation from Mr. Gorgeous will go very far in helping you land a job."

I guzzle my entire mug of wine and pour what's left in the bottle into my empty cup. "I don't really think I have a choice."

"Of course, you have a choice!" Gail replies fiercely. "He can't force you to go to Hawaii and pretend to be married to him."

I stare at the liquid in my mug. "He said if I don't do it, he won't be able to stop the company from laying me off. And if I'm let go, the money I owe them will have to be collected immediately."

This news brings a hush over the room, until the silence is interrupted by Gail's gasp. "You have to do it. You have to go to Hawaii and pretend to be his wife. And then, right when Miss Celebrity Whisperer is on the brink of getting that scoop, you have to flip the switch!"

"Yes!" Jen agrees enthusiastically through her mouthful of chocolate crème.

"Flip what switch?" I ask, thoroughly confused as Knickknack enters the kitchen. "What the hell is that smell?"

"That's Nicki," Jen replies casually, using her nickname for the dog. "The cheaper kibble is giving him a little bit of gas."

I cover my nose to block out the smell. "You call that a little bit?"

Gail continues with her original train of thought undaunted. "Once you're ready to get the scoop, you have to tell Logan you won't close the deal with Kitty and Jason unless he agrees to a larger raise, a complete wipe of your debt to Kensington, and a glowing recommendation letter. You know, should the company still go under."

Jen nods vigorously. "What's good for the goose, and all that."

I shake my head. "I don't know. That seems awfully risky. What if he calls my bluff and I lose everything?"

Jen cocks an eyebrow. "The man is willing to pretend to be married to get this scoop. He wouldn't do that unless he was desperate."

I consider this new proposition for a while as we

continue stuffing our faces with more Twinkies and wine. Finally, I come to the conclusion that they're right. If I'm going to risk my journalistic integrity for Logan Pierce, I'm going to have to make sure that I walk away from this with a future.

A smile spreads across my face as I lean back in my chair. "Okay. As soon as that scoop is within my grasp, I'm flipping the switch. Mr. Gorgeous won't know what hit him."

CHAPTER 3

LOGAN

I arrive at my father's Park Avenue penthouse twenty fashionable minutes late. As usual, I find Everett and his wife, Lindy, in the kitchen, sitting in the stools at the kitchen island, glasses of chilled white wine in hand as my father attempts to cook.

Lindy's long red hair is pulled into the usual tight bun resting atop the crown of her narrow head. Her usual pearl necklace is draped around her neck, accentuating her sharp collar bones and creamy white cardigan. Everett's dark hair is pulled back in that awful slicked back pompadour he's been unsuccessfully trying to pull off for three years. He's wearing his usual Brioni suit — minus the tie — in a dark charcoal color, to match the color of his soul, I presume.

Everett sets down his glass of wine and watches me as I enter. "Late, as usual," he remarks with a smirk.

I pat him on the back before I bump cheeks with his wife. "Please don't get up," I reply, hoping this will keep Lindy from attempting to get up to give me a proper hug.

Lindy is actually one of my former flings. Okay, one of my *many* former flings whom my brother has seen fit to swoop in and comfort after it didn't work out with me. I don't do commitment. Some women refuse to believe me when I tell them this. Lindy was one of those.

Needless to say, Lindy and Everett hit it off and despite their seemingly perfect marriage, Lindy still likes to get a bit touchy with me. I am certain my brother is aware of Lindy's wandering hands, but he pretends not to notice. Everett has never been good with the ladies. Negging is the only tool in his arsenal.

A slim brunette stands next to my father, accepting tastes of whatever sauce he's slaving over. She appears to be at least twenty years his junior. This must be my father's new fiancée, whom he spoke of the other day. One glance is all it takes for me to know she's not in this for my dad's terrible cooking.

"It's good to see you," I say, patting his shoulder. "And who might I ask are you, young lady?"

The brunette chuckles, flashing me a coquettish

smile. "Oh, aren't you such a charmer. You must be Logan. I've heard *so* much about you."

"I'm sure you have," I say, pulling a grape off the fruit plate on the counter and popping it in my mouth.

She holds out her hand for a shake. "I'm Priscilla," she says, taking my hand in both of hers and squeezing. "But everyone calls me Prissy."

Of course they do, I think.

Lindy and Prissy and Everett and Jasper. Sometimes, I feel a strong urge to bring home a beautiful ethnic woman with an exotic name, just to see the pearl-clutching and scandalized looks on their faces.

"So you two are engaged to be married?" I inquire as I pour myself a glass of wine.

Prissy beams as she plants a red imprint of her puckered lips on my father's wrinkled cheek. "We're getting married New Year's Eve."

I nearly choke on my wine. "New Year's Eve? That's less than two months away."

Not only was New Year's Eve less than two months away, it also happened to be my mother and father's wedding anniversary — when they were still married, of course. I always knew my dad was a sadist, but this is a whole new level of callous.

"Yes, brother, very astute of you to notice," Everett comments dryly while Lindy stares at me, running her tongue along the edge of her teeth absentmindedly, as if lost in thoughts of all the times she ran that tongue along my dick.

I shake my head. "Don't you think this is a bit... Oh, what's the word...fast?"

Not to mention in very poor taste.

Lindy chimes in. "How would you know, Logan? When it comes to you and relationships, everything is fast."

I ignore Lindy's jibe and address my father again. "Dad, you don't think this is a bit hasty?"

My father covers the sauce pot with a lid and sets down his wooden spoon before he looks me in the eye. "Son, I've been divorced for seven years. I have known Prissy for more than two years, as the daughter of my caddie."

My eyebrows shoot up. "The daughter of your caddie?" I remark. "I guess fetching my father's balls runs in the family."

"Logan!" my father shouts as Maria, his plump housekeeper, enters the kitchen. He quickly uses her as an excuse to change the subject. "Maria, can you please set the table in the dining room? And fetch that 2002 bottle of Dom Perignon from the cellar, please. Tonight, we're celebrating."

Maria nods. "Yes, Mr. Pierce."

"Thank you, dear," my father says, turning back to me. "As I was saying, Prissy and I have known each other for quite some time. Yes, we began seeing each other romantically just a few months ago, but you can't put a timeline on love. We're getting married New Year's Eve, and I want you to be there, Logan. I'll even allow you to bring whatever poor girl you're dating at the time."

All eyes are on me. It is no secret that I'm closer to my mother than I am to my father. Though my parents waited to divorce until after I graduated from Yale, right before I began law school, their marriage had been pretty much over since somewhere around the time I hit puberty. In fact, I was twelve years old the first time I saw my father with another woman.

"I'll have to think about it," I remark.

I'm halfway through my trout, and Prissy and my father's third retelling of how he proposed to her, when I can no longer keep my mouth shut. "Did you invite Mom to the wedding?" I ask as I slice off a piece of carrot and pop it in my mouth.

Prissy flashes me a look of pure exasperation before turning her attention back to her meal.

My father shakes his head as he pours himself some more champagne. "I am sure the last place your mother would want to be this New Year is at my wedding."

"You're well aware I have no intention of leaving her to ring the New Year in alone," I reply, grabbing the champagne bottle and pouring the last dregs into my glass.

My father waves off my suggestion. "By all means, Logan, spend your pathetic New Year's with your mother again."

My father knows all too well that the reason I spend every New Year's Eve with my mother is because I don't want her to spend it alone with her many years of equally happy and awful anniversary memories. By the time my parents divorced seven years ago, my mother was in her fifties. She lives a quiet life at her estate in Southampton now, where she has a few goats, a horse, some chickens, and a couple of dogs to keep her company. But every year, I battle many horrendous hours of New Year's Eve traffic through freezing rain and snow to keep her company.

My father drains his champagne glass and sets it down. "Isn't it about time you got married yourself, Logan?"

I look around at my dinner companions and everyone else seems to be avoiding eye contact with me, though my father is looking me straight in the eye. "Actually, funny you should bring that up," I reply, relishing the look of surprise on Everett and Lindy's faces. "You may begin hearing some rumors about my marital status over the next week or so, as I begin working to bring *Close-Up* magazine out of the red. Don't believe everything you hear."

Everett cocks one of his thick black eyebrows. "I do believe father said you're not allowed to sleep with anyone to win the shares. That would probably also entail *marrying* someone to win the shares."

"Actually, there was no mention about marriage," I reply smugly. "But don't fret, brother. I have no intention of marrying someone to win my shares."

Everett laughs. "*Your* shares? That's some bravado."

I shake my head and lean back in my chair. "It's not bravado. It's confidence. It's easy to be confident when you don't have to bribe people to do what you want."

My father lets out a hearty laugh, his face flushed from all the alcohol. "Well, boys, there'll be plenty of time to fight over who wins later. You both have until December tenth to save *Close-Up* and *Open Sky* from certain death. After that, I will be the judge of who is the better businessman. And I will announce my decision at the company Christmas party on December fifteenth."

If history had taught me anything, I'm certain my father and Everett are both expecting me to fail. But I have a few tricks up my sleeve – namely my sexy little celebrity whisperer who's deeply indebted to Kensington. If all goes according to plan, and my assistant Nora did her research on Sophie properly, I'm going to get a celebrity scoop to trump all celebrity scoops. I'm going to send *Close-Up* magazine out of the red and skyrocketing into the black.

I glance at Everett and he looks very confident with this news of a deadline. "Like I said, you may start hearing rumors about me getting married sometime in the near future. Don't believe everything you hear." I drain my glass of champagne and set it down gently before I rise from the table and clap Everett on the shoulder. "Let the games begin."

CHAPTER 4

SOPHIE

I shove the shower curtain open before leaving the bathroom, one of my many girl rituals. I figure if I ever come home to find my shower curtain has been pulled closed, I'll know it's because there's a serial killer hiding in my tub waiting to ambush me. I never realized how living alone in the three-bedroom house in Brooklyn where I grew up would make me so paranoid.

I feel guilty admitting I had assumed that, after my father succumbed to ALS — also referred to as Lou Gehrig's disease or amyotrophic lateral sclerosis — I would suddenly have a glamorous lifestyle, *ala* Carrie Bradshaw. Just a simple girl writing simple gossip articles and hosting glamorous parties. I didn't anticipate that I would become so depressed after my father's death that I would gain ten pounds and start rejecting most social invitations.

I also didn't anticipate I would find myself agreeing to fake-marry someone just to hold onto the last piece of my father I have left.

I pour myself a glass of water from the tap and chug it down, as I glance around the kitchen where my mom used to make my favorite cowboy spaghetti. I run my hand along the orange Formica countertop as I study the wood cabinets that my father never got around to refinishing before he passed. His final words to me, as he sailed down the Morphine River into the great unknown, were, "Shortcake, this is your home now. It's okay if you don't want to stay here." Then, he was gone.

He's been gone almost two years and I haven't worked up the courage to call a real estate agent nor break out the sandpaper and primer to refinish the cabinets. The eight buckets of paint and wood stain stacked up in the basement continue to collect dust. Sort of like my heart.

Sometimes, it's easier to let something precious fall into disrepair. When you dust things off and shine them up, you run the risk of catching a glimpse of your own reflection. Then, you might have to own up to the fact that you get paid to gossip about people's private lives.

Not to mention, I might look in the mirror and

realize I actually prefer myself as a blonde. I definitely can't let Logan know that.

My phone vibrates in my pocket, startling me out of my pensive mood. Sliding the phone out, I get an unmistakable sensation of butterflies fluttering in my belly as the sight of Logan's name catches me off guard. I feel like a pubescent teenager answering a call from the coolest guy in school. It's been a long time since any man has elicited that feeling in me.

"Hello?" I answer.

"I'm on my way. Should be there in about twenty minutes or so. Traffic on the parkway is —"

"You can't come here!" I blurt out "My neighbors *cannot* see us together."

Logan is silent for a moment. "What's wrong with your neighbors? Are they the nosey type?"

I sigh with frustration as I realize I foolishly assumed we would be riding to the airport separately, despite the fact that's not how married couples usually travel. "I've lived in this house since I was eleven years old," I reply. "I know *all* my neighbors. They all adored my father, so they check up on me often. They *know* I am not married. I can't lie to them about this."

He laughs. "Okay, so how am I going to pick you up?"

I begin making my way to my bedroom. "I'll meet you at your place. Just text me the address."

Silence again, but this time it's longer "Is this some

sort of ploy to get my address so you can start stalking me? I've never given out my address to a woman."

I pause at the entrance to my bedroom. "Are you kidding me right now?"

He chuckles again. "Okay, fine. I'll send you my address, but don't share it with anyone…and don't be late. Our flight leaves for Hawaii in less than two hours."

I end the call and drag my pale-blue leather suitcase — the one my father used for nearly two decades — down the stairs. It bumps along behind me and nearly bowls me over. I lose my grip on the handle and the suitcase goes clattering down the wooden stairs. With a loud thud, it lands on the wood floor at the bottom of the steps.

I hurry after it, snatching my handbag out of the coat closet near the front door. Standing just inside the threshold, I summon an Uber and go out onto my front stoop to wait for its arrival. Within a few minutes, a silver Toyota Corolla pulls up to the curb.

The guy driving the Uber has a long beard that reaches his chest, and he makes no attempt to get out of his vehicle and help me with my luggage. I drag the suitcase down the steps, one at a time, being careful not to let the suitcase gain too much momentum. When I finally reach the sidewalk, a raindrop lands on my eyebrow.

I scurry toward the back of the Toyota and tap the

top of the trunk, indicating for the driver to pop it open. He doesn't seem to hear me over the electronic music blasting inside the car. I leave my suitcase and walk around to the driver's side window.

He looks up as if he's surprised to see me, then he turns down his music and lowers his window. "Did you call for an Uber, or what?"

I swallow my anger and point at the back of the car. "Can you open the trunk, please?"

He presses a button to pop the trunk, but makes no attempt to help me load my suitcase.

It takes a couple minutes to figure out how to slide it in without damaging the guy's car. There's no way I can lift it high enough to drop it inside. Finally, I decide I don't give a shit and I lean it against the bumper and slide that baby in with no protection.

Slamming the trunk closed, I get into the back seat and angrily slam the door shut.

"You moving out or something?" the guy asks as he pulls away from the curb.

I want to ignore his question. He didn't help me with my luggage, so he doesn't really have a right asked me such a personal question. But I really don't want to anger this inconsiderate man whose car smells a bit like blue cheese.

"No," I reply simply.

I hope my abrupt response will deliver a strong hint that I do not want chat. But I have no such luck.

"You going to a hotel or something?" Mr. Nosey Parker asks. "Seems like an awful big suitcase just to go across town. Got a body in there?"

So he *did* see me struggling with the suitcase.

"I'm just making a stop before I head to the airport," I reply, trying to keep my answer as brief as possible.

I doubt this guy keeps up with the Manhattan social scene enough to know who Logan Pierce is. And I'm positive he doesn't recognize my name on my Uber profile as the byline on countless *Close-Up* articles. But you can never be too certain. And absolutely no one can know who I am or what I'm doing with Logan this week. Nevertheless, I will be filing a worker's compensation claim as soon as we get back from the retreat, for the damage done to my hair by bleaching it blonde – so I more closely resemble Logan's "type." *Gag.*

The guy smiles as he picks his nose and turns right onto the parkway, such a multitasker. "I can take you to the airport. You know, if you're not going to be at this place for too long. I can wait a few minutes."

I have a friend who drives an Uber, so I know this guy gets paid better on longer trips versus shorter trips. I know he's just trying to make a living. But it's not my job to pad his paycheck. If he wanted a little extra out of this trip, he should have dug into his human decency reserve instead of his nostrils.

"No, thanks. I won't need a ride to the airport."

"Aw, come on! I don't mind waiting a few minutes. I can take you to the airport. Come on, I'm trying to save up money to buy my daughter a computer for school. Come on."

This ride has suddenly gotten very awkward. First, the guy doesn't want to help me with my luggage. Now, he wants me to reward his stellar customer service by agreeing to allow him to drive me to the airport when I have clearly said I don't need a ride.

I swallow hard and shift uncomfortably in my seat. "Look, I'm really sorry, but I don't need a ride. My... friend is giving me a ride. But thank you for offering. I hope your daughter gets her computer soon."

The driver shakes his head in dismay, but he doesn't reply. The rest of the twelve-minute ride is filled with complete and utter awkward silence. By the time we pull up to Logan's Park Avenue apartment building, my hand is on the door handle, and I'm ready to jump out as soon as the vehicle comes to a stop. Which is exactly what I do, despite the fact a valet is approaching the car with the clear intention of opening the door for me.

"Oh, I'm fine. Thank you," I assure the valet. "We don't need parking. I'm just being dropped off."

The young, clean-cut valet with the stunning smile and wide brown eyes flashes me a bright smile. "Of course, let me help you with your bag, ma'am," he says as the driver pops the trunk.

"Thank you so much," I gush.

Even the strapping young valet has a bit of a task pulling the suitcase out of the trunk. "My pleasure, ma'am. Not"—*grunt*—"a problem."

I slam the trunk closed and glance back at the silver Corolla as I walk away.

The driver glares at me as he lowers the passenger window. "I knew you wouldn't tip me!"

I point my finger at him. "Yeah, well, maybe you'd get a tip if you cleaned your car!" I turn around and practically smash my face into Logan's rock-hard chest. "Oh! I didn't see you there."

Logan cocks an eyebrow as a bellman comes out to assist with my suitcase, taking it to the back of a black Range Rover parked behind the Corolla. "Certainly don't travel light, do you?"

I can smell him at this distance, and the scent is oddly comforting: warm, spicy, with a hint of freshly-pressed linen and aged leather. Smells like money. I look up at his perfectly-styled dark hair, his chiseled face with just the right amount of scruff, his expensive suit. He smells like money because he *is* money.

What the hell am I doing here?

Unlike the Uber driver from hell, the chauffeur who takes us to the airport is silent the entire ride. He doesn't ask us to donate to his cause or refuse to help us with our luggage. Why...it's almost as if having money changes a person.

As pleasant as my experience is with Logan's chauffeur, and the priority service we receive when we check in for our first class flight to Hawaii, it only serves to magnify the differences between Logan and me. We come from two different worlds. I'll have to keep reminding myself of that. I can't forget for a single moment that Logan Pierce is only in this for himself.

———

As we take our seats in row two of the first-class cabin, I begin to feel almost like a bit of a fugitive. It seems criminal to sit in such a comfortable, spacious leather seat, being served drinks before the flight even takes off. Meanwhile, my fellow passengers in coach are struggling to cram their knees in and silently hoping the open seat next to them stays empty for the rest of the flight.

Logan watches me as I guzzle the tiny complimentary bottle of water. "You look like a homeless person trying to consume as much food as you can at the salad bar before you get kicked out. There's more water where that came from. Have you never flown first class?"

I narrow my eyes at him. "That was actually very

insulting. You do realize that, don't you?"

He stares at me blankly, totally oblivious to the way he so easily stokes my inferiority complex.

I shake my head. "Yes, this is my first time flying first class, which apparently is very obvious. Thank you for reminding me."

That sexy laugh spills out of his perfect mouth. "So you're telling me," he begins, his elbow nudging mine softly, "that I'm responsible for popping your first class cherry?"

I turn in my seat, so my entire body is facing him. "Listen here," I begin, ignoring the sly smirk on his face. "I've given this whole couples retreat thing a lot of thought over the last few days."

He tilts his head curiously. "And what did you come up with, Miss Celebrity Whisperer?"

I smile at his attempt to stroke my ego. "Exactly. I think it would do you well to remember that *I* am the one with the skill to pull this off."

His elbow nudges mine again as he leans in close enough for me to feel his body heat. "So you think that I am somehow *unskilled* at making people do whatever I want them to do?" His eyes are locked on mine as his fingertip grazes the top of my hand.

I swallow hard as I suddenly feel my heartbeat pulsing in every — and I do mean *every* — part of my body. "Oh, I know you can get people to do what you want," I reply, shaking my head as I pull my hand back. "Everyone in New York knows how you do that."

He rolls his eyes. "You're starting to sound like my father."

I nod in agreement before I catch myself. "Your father? Actually, never mind your father. Stop trying to change the subject. Back to that other thing."

He smiles. "What other thing?"

"You know what I'm talking about," I reply, pointing an accusatory finger at him. "Your ability to get people to do what you want. There will be none of *that*. I have four rules for this trip."

He chuckles. "*Rules*? You have got to be kidding me."

"I'm serious as sweat socks."

"As *what*?"

"You know what I mean," I scoff.

He shakes his head. "And what might those four 'serious as sweat socks' rules be?"

I hand my empty water bottle to the flight attendant. "Rule number one," I begin, leaning in a little so I'm not overheard. "Absolutely no sex. Number two. No sleeping in the same bed."

Logan holds up a finger to stop me. "Wait a minute. Don't you think it will be a bit suspicious if we show up at a couples retreat asking for a room with two beds? Married couples sleep together."

I stick out my chin, ready with an answer. "I've

already thought of that. This is a tantric intimacy retreat for couples who obviously have shitty sex lives. There has to be a few, maybe even as many as *half* of the couples, who don't sleep together anymore."

He ponders this for a long moment before he seems to decide he can't argue. "Okay, seems you have this figured out. So what are rules three and four?"

I draw in a deep breath and let it out slowly. "Number three: No skinny-dipping or nudity of any kind. And number four: No discussing my parents."

He scrunches his eyebrows in confusion at this fourth rule. "You do realize that we'll have to take part in mandatory therapy sessions at this retreat, and I have no control over what kinds of questions the therapist will ask you about your parents."

I cock an eyebrow. "You're a rich, powerful, charming man. You said it yourself, you're very good at getting people to do what you want. I'm sure you can figure out a way to tip off the therapist on what topics are off-limits."

He nods an agreement, pressing his lips together as he seems to think about my proposed four rules. "Okay. I can handle those four rules, but you have to agree to just one in return."

"Hit me."

"One rule to rule them all. And that rule is, you cannot blame me when you suddenly want to break your rule number one."

I throw my head back with laughter. "I am *not* having sex with you, Logan."

He smiles as the flight attendant arrives with his glass of champagne. "We'll see about that."

I point at the champagne bottle in the woman's hands. "Are those drinks really free?"

Logan nods, smiling as he watches my champagne being poured, and I throw back the entire glass of in a couple of gulps. "I guess I know how you'll be keeping yourself occupied during this eleven-hour flight."

"You should probably use this time to read the questionnaire I emailed you and your attorney this morning. You know, the one asking me all those personal questions, like what brand of tampons I use."

He chuckles again, and the sound feels like a whisper of fingertips gliding over my skin. "Well, what brand is it?"

I shake my head. "Nuh-uh. You have to do your own homework. Did you send me your questionnaire?"

He smiles. "I did. I'm sure you'll be very pleased to find out what brand of condom I prefer. I'll give you a hint, it begins with Magnum and ends with extra-large."

I smile as I attempt to appear unfazed despite the loud thumping of my heartbeat echoing inside my ears. "Perfect. Just like my tampons."

His laughs loudly and with total abandon.

"Speaking of things you put your fingers inside," he says, reaching into his breast pocket and retrieving two gold wedding bands and a ring with the biggest diamond I've ever seen. "We should put these on before we land."

I take the two smaller rings and slide them both onto my left ring finger, my eyes widening with shock at how heavy the diamond feels. "If this plane goes down, it will be this thing's fault."

He slides on his faux wedding band and leans back in his seat. "Till death do us part, wifey."

Once the plane has taken off, I assume we will each retire to the comfort of our reading material. But as luck would have it, Logan doesn't seem to have brought anything to read.

"So how do you like working at *Close-Up*?" he asks after the flight attendant takes our lunch order.

"I love it!" I reply enthusiastically. "It's my dream job. Exactly what I imagined myself doing when I majored in journalism."

He shakes his head. "Is there nothing about it you enjoy?"

I shrug. "Actually, I love reading the comments on my articles."

He looks at me like I'm crazy. "More sarcasm?"

I shake my head adamantly. "Nope. Sometimes, I pour myself a glass of wine and read the comments aloud in Morgan Freeman's voice."

"In Morgan Freeman's voice?" he replies, obviously impressed. "Well, now you have to demonstrate this talent."

I draw in a deep breath as I slide the *Skymall* catalog out of the leather pocket on the back of the seat in front of me and begin reading in my best Morgan Freeman voice. "LyxPro noise-cancelling Bluetooth headphones. Professional sound meets the freedom of hands-free. Rediscover portable listening pleasure."

His jaw drops as he stares at me. "That is both the worst Morgan Freeman impression and the sexiest thing I have ever heard in my life."

"I never said it was good," I say, sliding the catalog back into the leather pocket while trying desperately to ignore how he just called me sexy.

He shakes his head. "No, it wasn't good. It was awful, and strangely arousing. I am one proud hubby."

I roll my eyes as I reach into my pocket to retrieve my phone. "I'm going to read a book now. Let me know if you'd like me to read aloud to keep you entertained."

"I'll pass. There is such thing as too much of a good thing. We have to save some of the fun for the retreat," he says with a ridiculously sexy grin.

I turn my body away from him to keep myself myself from stealing glances at those large hands and perfect lips. "I can hardly wait."

CHAPTER 5

LOGAN

*O*ur driver drops us off at the Paradise Tantra Resort in Honolulu. The retreat is actually located inside a Hilton hotel. When we pull into the porte-cochère, a representative of the retreat checks us into the hotel using an iPad then directs us to an outdoor bell desk. The desk and the pathway leading to the hotel entrance are all covered by overhead walkways, which is a good thing considering it is raining cats and dogs in Honolulu today.

Sophie shakes her head as a bellman lugs our bags out of the trunk and places them on a brass luggage cart while we head toward the outdoor bell desk. "Hawaii in November? Who the hell goes to Hawaii in November?"

I place my hand on the small of her back to guide her forward as the bell desk attendant beckons us. She glances at my arm and clears her throat loudly, as if to signal that I'm breaking some sort of rule by touching her.

I slowly remove my hand as we arrive at the bell desk, then I lean in to whisper in her ear, "None of your rules said anything about touching. Nonetheless, I will respect your wishes."

The guy behind the counter flashes us a beaming smile. "Can I have your last name, sir?"

"Pierce. Logan Pierce," I reply leaning over the counter and lowering my voice to a conspiratorial whisper. "Do you think you can get us a room with *two* beds?"

The guy smiles at Sophie. "Good afternoon, Mrs. Pierce," he says before he turns his attention back to me as he hands me two card keys for the room. "I'm very sorry, Mr. Pierce, but the Paradise Tantra Resort has limited room availability and all our rooms have just one bed. This is meant to promote intimacy and togetherness while attending the resort. If this is an issue, we can—"

"You've *got* to be kidding me," Sophie interjects.

I place a gentle hand on her forearm. "It's okay, dear. I'm sure we can figure something out. After all, we are here to get *closer*, right?"

Sophie's nostrils flare as she forces a smile. "Right...closer."

Neither of us says a word as we follow the

bellman up to the twelfth floor, where all the Paradise Tantra Resort guests' rooms are located. I open the door to suite 1210 and pass the bellman a generous tip, which he thanks me for before he swiftly sets off toward the elevator. The maids' cart parked outside our suite is an eyesore. Though we checked in an hour before the resort's official check-in time, I suppose it's to be expected that the cleaning staff may not have finished their rounds. But when we enter the room, it appears squeaky clean and empty.

I let out a sigh of relief and plop down onto the sofa in the sitting area near the sliding glass door leading out to the balcony. "I'll sleep on the sofa. I wouldn't want to break any more of your rules."

"The rules are in place to keep us from messing this up," Sophie says as she heads toward the bathroom.

Before she can even touch the knob, the bathroom door swings inward and out walks a tiny Asian hotel maid. Both the lady and Sophie let out surprised gasps.

"Oh, I am so, so sorry," the maid apologizes profusely. "I was just finishing. Bathroom is clean now. Enjoy your stay. So sorry. I will leave now."

Sophie and I don't say a word as the woman leaves the hotel room, letting the door fall closed behind her.

Another gasp issues from Sophie's wide open

mouth as she spins around. "Do you think she heard us talking?"

I shrug. "I don't know, but does it really matter? It doesn't seem like she speaks very good English. It's not like she'll be able to infer we're here to spy on their celebrity guests by the simple mention of us having rules. Besides, she's an employee of the resort. It's her *job* to exercise discretion."

Sophie cocks an eyebrow. "Have you been paying attention at all?" she remarks incredulously. "We're here as spies for a *gossip* magazine. Believe me when I say I'm an expert at these things. Do you know how *easy* it is to bribe hotel staff or a disgruntled employee to get confidential information on a celebrity?"

I smile at her attempt to school me. "It's a good thing neither of us are celebrities."

"You do realize saying that aloud doesn't make it true? You're definitely a celebrity. And I'm on a lot of celebrity hit lists."

I laugh, perhaps a bit too hard based on the scathing looks she shoots me. "You dyed your hair blonde, and you're using the last name Pierce. Everyone at the office thinks you haven't been to work this week because I put you on paid administrative leave when I called you into my office on Monday," I say, rising from the sofa and slowly making my way toward her so I don't have to shout across the room. "As for me, everyone thinks I'm on a 'business trip' in

China. No one in New York is going to suspect we're at a couples retreat in Honolulu together. No one is looking for us. So chill, okay?"

She draws in a long, deep breath, then lets it out slowly, looking up at me as I step into her personal space. "You'd better be right, because if our cover is blown, the last bit of journalistic integrity I've managed to hold onto while working at *Close-Up* will slip through my fingers."

My smiles fades as I suddenly realize I hold this woman's fate in my hands. "I won't let that happen," I say, my gaze locked on her striking blue eyes. "I promise."

She's frozen for a moment, then she swallows hard and spins around. "I just need to freshen up, then we can go down and have dinner before the welcoming ceremony."

"Welcoming ceremony?" I remark, reaching for the resort brochure on the desk as the bathroom door closes behind her. "What exactly does that entail? Do we have to sacrifice our sex toys to a volcano or something?"

"I don't know," Sophie shouts through the door. "The description in the brochure and on the website is very vague."

I unfold the brochure and read the list of activities.

· · ·

DAY ONE:

8 p.m. - Welcoming Ceremony and first council meeting

DAY TWO:

9 a.m. - 12 p.m. - One-on-one intake session
2 p.m. - Exploring Tantric Intimacy
8 p.m. - Council meeting

IT APPEARS we will be having a busy week. Days three, four, and five are packed with cringe-inducing activities, with day six culminating in something vaguely referred to as "declarations" followed by another council meeting. Looking at this itinerary, I doubt we'll make it through the week without fucking or murdering each other.

Sophie emerges from the bathroom looking fresh-faced and ready take on the world. Her shoulders are pulled back as she wears an expression of confidence and determination. Not to mention, she is fucking gorgeous in an understated way. It's apparent she has no idea how beautiful she is, which is both sad and perfect. Because any woman who would agree to marry me would have to be out of their fucking mind or completely undervaluing themselves.

I can't help but look her up and down before I

speak. "Well, I don't know about you, but I'm starving," I begin. "And it seems we have a few hours to kill before the welcoming ceremony. I say we go down and grab some dinner and drinks."

She shakes her head. "No drinks. I had enough of those on the plane. But I could use a giant steak."

"If it's a big piece of meat you're craving…" I laugh as she rolls her eyes. "Are you ready for our first council meeting, dear?"

"I'm ready if you are, hubby."

At her words, a weird sensation of warmth floods my chest. The idea of marriage normally makes me sweat or cringe, or both. But hearing her say the word "hubby" fills me with a strange sense of pride, and I find myself grinning like a fucking idiot.

"What?" she asks, glancing down at her outfit of white jean shorts and a turquoise T-shirt, which she's tied at her waist.

I chuckle as I tear my gaze away from her. "Nothing. You… You look good, Soph."

"Soph?" she replies.

I shake my head as I reach for the door handle. "You look beautiful, *dear*."

She narrows her stunning hazel eyes at me as I hold the door open for her. "Yeah, well, you'd…you'd better keep those hands where I can see them at all times."

I lean in to whisper in her ear. "I'll keep my hands

to myself, as long as you know that I'm willing to put my hands wherever *you* want them...anytime."

She rolls her eyes. "I'll keep that in mind."

THE RECREATION AREA of the Hilton Hotel, used by the Paradise Tantra Resort for group activities and council meetings, is a large circular expanse of grass surrounded by paved pathways leading to and from the hotel and the beach. The edges of the grass are lined with palm trees and throngs of passing tourists. It looks like a park you'd find in your average sun-drenched American city, but the one-hundred-eighty-degree views of the sparkling blue Pacific Ocean sets it apart.

A covered, wooden gazebo stands in the middle of the recreation area, which is probably used for ridiculously expensive weddings when it's not being used by miserable married couples. It's almost as if the resort is drumming up their own business. At least we'll have shelter from the rain.

The rest of the couples are gathered around and appear to be awkwardly introducing themselves to one another. One man with a ginger beard down to his chest looks downright pissed off. Most of the couples appear to be in their forties, fifties, and sixties. The only couple that seems to be as young as Sophie and me are Kitty and Jason.

Kitty's jet-black hair is pulled up in a high ponytail, and from a hundred feet away I can see her trademark bright-orange lipstick. Jason stands next to her, his enormous ex-NFL player body towering over Kitty protectively.

Sophie whispers to me out the side of her mouth as we climb the gazebo steps up. "Crazy eyes incoming."

The wrinkly, tanned woman barreling toward us with the crazy eyes flashes us a warm smile. "Come, come. We've been waiting for you," she declares, pushing us toward the gathering of couples in the center of the gazebo.

I glance at the time on my wristwatch in confusion. "We're five minutes early," I whisper to Sophie.

She holds her index finger in front of her shimmering lips to shush me. She nods to her right and I follow her lead as we slowly inch our way sideways until we're closer to Kitty and Jason.

"Aloha, couples," crazy eyes begins. "As most of you probably already know, I am Dr. Sharon Mahoe. And I am *very* happy to have you all here with us today. This gorgeous man standing next to me is my husband, Bobby."

Next to Dr. Mahoe stands a man who looks like a seven-foot-tall leather-skinned Vin Diesel, but I recognize him from the Paradise Tantra Resort website, so I'm not too taken aback. Next to him, Dr. Mahoe looks like an overly-tanned, middle-aged munchkin with curly brown hair that is quickly reaching Afro status in the sticky Hawaiian humidity. The floral sarong she wears shows a large section of her bare leg, which is decorated with henna tattoos I assume are meant to accentuate her varicose veins.

"Does everyone in Hawaii look like they're made of leather?" I mutter to Sophie.

"It's pretty sunny down here," she says, nodding toward Dr. Mahoe. "That woman is eleven years old."

Mahoe flashes me a severe look as I laugh out loud. "I know many of you are not exactly... enthusiastic about attending this retreat," she continues. "It's not easy to admit there's a problem in your marriage. But when the problem is of a sexual nature, it is often even more difficult to acknowledge. You are all extremely brave for being here today and recommitting yourselves to making your marriage work. So give yourselves and your partners a pat on the back. Go on!"

The couples awkwardly look around to see if anyone is actually doing anything, so I decide to take the lead. I pat myself on the back first, then I turn to Sophie and swat her gorgeous ass.

Her hazel eyes widen for a split second before she seems to remember we're supposed to be married. "Oh, you," she says with a smile, then she pretends to give me a gentle punch in the arm, but it's anything but gentle.

I smile as I rub my tricep. "I'll get you back for that…when you least expect it."

She shakes her head and nods toward Mahoe. "Pay attention, honey."

When I reluctantly turn my attention back to Dr. Mahoe, she's explaining the two rectangular hay bales stacked up behind her and Bobby. Secured to the front of top hay bale is a wooden target painted with a red and white bull's-eye. On the floor next to the hay are two woven baskets, one of which appears to be full of hatchets.

Mahoe begins pacing in front of the target as she continues to speak. "You are all here because you are on a spiritual quest for sexual empowerment," she begins. "I am going to guide you on your journey of discovery for the next six days, but it is *you* who must determine which path you will take when you return home to your looming mortgages and stressful careers and screaming children. Will you continue on the path to dissatisfaction and separateness? Or will you join me in taking the path to vulnerability, sensuality, and true intimacy?"

I glance at Sophie, and I'm not surprised to see the skeptical look on her face.

Mahoe reaches into the basket that doesn't appear to contain hatchets and comes up with a metal bowl.

She shakes it gently as she walks toward the nearest couple, a woman and man who appear to be in their fifties. The woman picks a folded piece of paper out of the bowl, and Mahoe quickly moves onto the next couple, leaving the husband with his hand hanging mid-air.

"Here at the Paradise Tantra Resort, we have a motto," Mahoe continues. "Find a little play in every day," she says as the next couple takes a folded slip of paper and she moves on. "Studies show that a couple who plays together stays together. So I am going to show you not just how to improve your sex life, but how to play with your partner. I want to remind you that you are a team."

She holds out the bowl to the next couple. "To maintain the spirit of playfulness, each couple will be given a tribal name. This will help you to feel like a team. It will also promote the sense of competition and feeling you are fighting for something, you are fighting to win, you are fighting for your marriage."

Next, she holds the bowl out to Kitty and Jason, and Jason takes the folded piece of paper, leaving two extra slips in the bowl. As Mahoe steps in front of Sophie and me with a maniacal smile on her face, I allow Sophie to take the piece of paper for us. I figure this has to earn me some good-husband points.

But Sophie doesn't acknowledge my attempt at chivalry. Like a good little gossip columnist, Sophie immediately turns to Kitty to ask her what their piece of paper says.

Kitty holds her up. "We got Ka'manu. It says it means *the bird* in Hawaiian," she says, not at all the type of response I would expect from a so-called prima donna.

Sophie stares at our slip of paper for a moment, looking like she suddenly regrets choosing this moment to engage Kitty. "We got…Ka'pipi. It says it means *the cow*." She turns to me and hands me the slip of paper. "Is this a bad omen?"

I stare at the words on the paper for a moment. "Honey, if you're a cow, that makes me a bull," I reply, using my index fingers to make fake horns on my head. "You'd better watch out tonight, or I might charge you with my big horns."

She shakes her head in dismay. "So now you have *two* horns? One for me and one for your mistress?"

I have to keep myself from laughing at this jilted wife act, but inside I'm dying. This woman is unlike anyone I've ever met. Not being able to touch her for the next six days is going to be torture.

Once we've all chosen our tribal names from the bowl, Dr. Mahoe hands out a few sheets of paper and a black marker to each couple. She asks us to write down the obstacles that are keeping us from achieving true intimacy in our marriages. Sophie makes me turn around so she can use my back as something hard to write on. When she's finished writing on her piece of paper, I ask her to turn around so I can do the same.

"You need something hard to write on?" she asks, then she reaches into the pocket of her shorts and pulls out a tube of lip balm.

"What the hell is that?

She grins. "Lip balm is very hard to write on."

I can't help but chuckle at this ridiculously awful joke. "That was a terrible Dad-joke."

She shrugs. "It was one of my dad's favs. Besides, she told us we have to play with each other. I'm just trying to follow Dr. Mahoe's path."

I glance at the tiny sliver of her midriff that's showing under the knot at the bottom of her T-shirt. "I can think of some funner ways we can play together."

She smiles. "Talented as you may be, in theory or reality, you know the rules," she says, turning her back to me. "Go ahead, write rule number one on your paper."

I laugh as I lay my sheet of paper over the top of her back. "I should have seen that one coming," I reply as I write in big block letters: DISINTEREST IN LOVEMAKING.

When she turns around and reads the words on the paper, she scrunches up her nose as if she's caught a whiff of something foul. "Lovemaking? You're going to make us both look like prudes."

"What does your say?"

She shows me the piece of paper where she wrote the word TRUST in letters twice the size of mine. "You know, because of your womanizing ways. I'm just *so* jealous."

Dr. Mahoe asks us one-by-one to attach the pieces of paper to the target. Each couple is supposed to throw their hatchets at the target to symbolize a declaration of war on "the barriers to true intimacy."

Mahoe stands behind the couples, while her seemingly mute husband stands on the grass — in the pouring rain — behind the area of the gazebo where the hay is stacked up. He has the important job of retrieving stray hatchets. He seems completely unfazed as hatchets fly by his head. He even catches one midair.

Four other couples go first, with only Kitty and Jason behind us. When it's our turn, it takes just one attempt for Sophie to land her hatchet on the first T in TRUST. The couples clap and cheer at her accuracy.

Dr. Mahoe approaches her and places her hands on Sophie's shoulders. "Good job, Ka'pipi!"

I press my lips together to keep from laughing until Mahoe is out of earshot. "Good job, Ka'pipi," I whisper to Sophie.

Mahoe digs her hand into the basket from which she retrieved the metal bowl earlier. This time she comes up with a small clay pot no larger than her palm. She makes her way back to Sophie, and I can see now the pot is filled with a black, glossy substance. She dips two fingers into it and swipes them across Sophie's cheeks.

War paint. This woman is brilliant.

"You are now a warrior for the Ka'pipi tribe. You have declared war on your trust issues."

More like this entire resort has declared war on my Ka'pipi, I want to say.

When it's my turn to throw my hatchet at the words DISINTEREST IN LOVEMAKING, my second throw lands dead center on the word *in*. My accuracy elicits more cheers from the other couples as I walk toward the target to remove the hatchet.

Arriving at the target, I wrap my fingers around the handle of the hatchet and hear a loud gasp, which is followed by a whoosh of air and a powerful thud between my legs. I glance downward and see a hatchet stuck in the hay bale just below my crotch.

I take a step back and slowly turn around to see who threw it. Kitty is standing a few feet away from Sophie, her hands covering her mouth. Sophie on the other hand, seems to be trying very hard not to laugh.

"I'm so sorry!" Kitty cries, racing toward me, with Jason right behind her. "I was just trying to aim, but it slipped from my grasp. I'm so sorry."

"Are you okay?" Jason asks.

"I'm fine!" I assure them, plastering a big smile across my face. "Really, it didn't even touch me."

After a few more profuse apologies from Kitty, I head back to join my tribe.

Sophie smiles as I approach her with my piece of paper. "Will you be needing to downsize from a Magnum extra-large now?"

"Very funny," I reply, as Dr. Mahoe makes her way toward me with her pot of war paint. "My Magnum is safe and sound, but I think my balls may have crawled up inside me."

After the hatchet throwing exercise, when all the couples have been anointed with war paint, Dr. Mahoe begins to explain the council meeting, which will take place every evening.

"The purpose of the council meeting is not to vote anyone off the island," Dr. Mahoe begins with a chuckle. "The purpose of the meeting is to recognize the tribe that has shown the most effort. So you cannot vote for anyone in your tribe, and the council meeting will force you to be present during the retreat. You will have to observe not only your own partner, but the other tribes as well. You may learn more from them than me! So go ahead and take one of your extra pieces of paper and write the name of the tribe that showed the most effort today. Then, fold your paper and put it in this bowl. I will come around to collect your votes."

When Mahoe is finished collecting our votes, she holds up each slip of paper to show us what is written as Bobby's head looks as if it will explode at any moment from having to keep tally. Six pieces of paper result in one vote for Kitty and Jason's Ka'manu tribe — that was our vote — and five votes for Ka'pipi tribe.

"The tribe that has overwhelmingly claimed today's title of Wedded Warriors is Ka'pipi!"

All the couples turn to us as they clap and cheer. Instinctively, I pick Sophie up and kiss her on the cheek. Sophie's eyes widen as she automatically tries to push me away. I set her down quickly to prevent anyone from noticing her reaction.

"Good job, Logan!" a male voice shouts from behind us.

I whip my head around to see Everett and Lindy in their best Hawaiian tourist outfits, approaching us with enormous grins on their faces. "Everett? What are you doing here?" The moment the words come out of my mouth, I remember that there was one extra slip of paper in the bowl when we chose tribal names.

Lindy immediately turns her attention to Dr. Mahoe. "Sharon, I'm so sorry we're late," she gushes. "I hope we didn't inconvenience you or any of the other couples."

Sharon? Lindy's on a first-name basis with Dr. Mahoe?

"Oh, nonsense, Lindy," Mahoe proclaims as Bobby hands his wife something that looks like a couple of necklaces. "I was just about to award the passion amulets to tonight's Wedded Warriors."

Lindy clasps her hands together and does an excited little hop. "Oh, perfect! Please carry on."

Dr. Mahoe approaches us and places a leather necklace around both my and Sophie's necks. I take a quick glance at the carved wooden amulet dangling from the thin strip of dark leather, and my eyes nearly pop out of their sockets. The carving appears to depict two turtles sixty-nining each other so their bodies form a yin and yang symbol.

"Ka'pipi, you will have a sensual treat awaiting you in your suite tonight," Dr. Mahoe says with a wink. "I will see you all tomorrow at nine a.m. for Tantra yoga. Aloha and good night, everyone."

"ALREADY IMPRESSING the other couples with your sham marriage, are you, brother?" Everett remarks as we make our way back to the hotel elevator.

I glance around to make sure none of the other couples heard him, and it seems the coast is clear. "If you've come here to sabotage me, you can think again. I have contingency plans in place," I reply, punching the call button on the elevator and trying to ignore the panicked expression on Sophie's face.

"Is that a threat? Do you have some compromising

material on standby, ready to be delivered to Father at a moment's notice?" Everett goads me.

"Sabotage my operation and you'll find out," I reply simply as the elevator doors slide open and we all bump into each other in an attempt to enter at the same time.

Everett scoffs as I take a step back so he and Lindy can enter first, then I grab Sophie's hand to keep her from entering.

Everett laughs as he realizes we're not getting in with them. "You can't hide from me forever!" he shouts as the doors slide shut.

After a tense but silent elevator ride up to our room, Sophie and I enter our suite to find a room service cart. Resting on top is an ice bucket filled with two bottles of champagne and a plate covered in a silver domed lid.

"Did you know your brother was coming?" Sophie demands, rounding on me with fury in her narrowed eyes.

"Of course not!" I reply. "He's just trying to throw me off my game so I screw this up."

"Why is he trying to screw this up? Is this some kind of innocent sibling rivalry thing or are you blackmailing him, too?"

"I'm not blackmailing you," I shoot back.

She rolls her eyes. "Oh, yeah, I forgot it's extortion, or bribery, or whatever. You're dangling a carrot, promising to make my most pressing problems go away. Do you think I don't know why you chose me? You probably asked your assistant to find the most desperate person in the office to help you with this stunt. I know how guys like you work."

"Guys like me?" I reply, trying to steer the subject away from her very accurate description of how I chose her for this job.

Sophie's debt to the company wasn't the only reason I chose her. Nevertheless, asking my assistant to investigate my new employees — to find someone who would be easy to manipulate — makes me look very bad. My other reasons for choosing Sophie, noble or not, are easily eclipsed by the gross invasion of privacy.

"Yes, guys like you," she replies defiantly. "Guys who think everything and every*one* has a price."

I laugh and shake my head at her assessment of me. "Sweetheart, you have no clue what you're talking about."

"Oh, really?" she challenges me. "When was the last time someone said no to you?"

I stare at her for a while as I search my brain for a reply, someone who may have recently turned me down for a business meeting or even a date. Then, I smile as the obvious answer comes to me. "You."

"What about me?"

"Your rules. All four of those rules. It's just a list of things I can't do."

She stares at me for a while, trying to come up with a response, but she settles on, "I mean, someone other than me."

I laugh again. "Can we forget about my brother? I want to find out what the hell is under that lid," I say, flashing her my most charming smile as I nod toward the room service cart. "I promise we can discuss this once I've had a glass of champagne."

She rolls her eyes. "Have your brother and his wife been to this resort before? They seemed awfully chummy with Dr. Mahoe."

"M'ho's intimate with everyone," I reply, and she responds by reaching into the bucket and throwing an ice cube at me.

"What's under the lid?" she asks.

"Maybe it's Dr. Sharon Mahoe's guide to sharin' your hos. You can check. I have to drain the weasel," I reply as I head toward the bathroom. I take a quick piss and when I emerge from the bathroom, Sophie is standing next to the room service cart holding an enormous pink dildo in her hand. "Well, you certainly decided to break rule number one very quickly."

She picks something up off the plate, which looks like another brochure.

"What's that?" I ask.

"It's a brochure of Tantric sex poses," Sophie

replies plainly. "This and the champagne and the dildo are our 'sensual treat.'"

I grab a bottle of champagne from the bucket as Sophie places the dildo and the brochure back on the plate. "Looks like we're going to have a wild night," I remark, just as the cork pops out of the champagne bottle and hits the ceiling.

Sophie flinches at the sound and casts me a scathing look. "Watch where you're pointing that thing. It was Kitty, not me, who almost chopped off your Ka'pipi."

I begin pouring her a glass of champagne, but when I try to hand it to her she shakes her head. "Suddenly you don't drink?"

"I told you, I had enough sauce on the plane," she replies as she unzips her suitcase and pulls out some clothing and a small zippered travel bag. "It's past nine. That means it's...past two a.m. in New York. I'm jetlagged. I just want to go to sleep."

"Don't forget to rinse your dentures before you put them on your nightstand," I tease her. "This is Hawaii. It's our first night here. Have a drink with me. I promise no funny stuff."

"You're on your own tonight, boss," she says as she stops in the doorway of the bathroom.

I set down my glass of champagne and make my way toward her. "I like it when you call me boss."

"Just don't let anyone from the resort see you out having drinks without me," she replies.

"You know, you're really more trusting than you made yourself out to be down there," I reply, getting in one last word before she closes the bathroom door behind her.

"Maybe that's because we're not really married," she says through the door.

I flinch as if she just opened a bottle of champagne in my face. But I don't flinch at her words. I flinch at my internal reaction to her words. Why does it hurt to be reminded that I'm not really married to this woman?

"You might want to keep your voice down," I reply, leaning closer to the door again. "Don't forget that everyone here thinks we're Wedded Warriors."

She doesn't reply, so I head back toward the room service cart to retrieve my glass of champagne. As I reach for it, I notice the gold wedding band on my finger. Sliding it off, I tuck it inside the breast pocket of my green Hawaiian shirt.

My mind fixates on the ring for a moment, and I realize I don't really want to go down and have a drink without Sophie. She's definitely the coolest person at this resort. Maybe even the whole damn island. Besides, I don't want anyone thinking we didn't appreciate Dr. Mahoe's "sensual treat."

Sophie emerges from the bathroom as I begin

removing the throw pillows from the couch to get ready for the worst sleep I've had since my frat days.

"What's that?" I ask.

"What's what?" she replies, placing the folded clothes she was wearing earlier in her open suitcase and zipping it up.

I head toward her to help move the suitcase off the bed. "That thing on your head," I reply, gently nudging her hand away so I can grab the leather handle.

"Oh, this? It's my pineapple," she replies casually.

"Your pineapple?" I say, easily lifting the suitcase and placing it on the luggage rack near the closet.

She seems dumbstruck for a brief moment before she replies, "Yes. If you were blessed with curly hair like me, you'd know what it is. At night, I pineapple my hair and sleep on a satin pillowcase to prevent frizz and breakage. But I forgot my pillowcase."

"Why didn't you tell me this before?"

She looks confused. "Why would I tell you about my pineapple?

"Because I need to know about your pineapple," I reply, trying not to stare at her gorgeous legs, which are barely covered by the oversized Yankees T-shirt she's wearing as a nightgown. "It wasn't in your questionnaire, but this is the stuff I need to know to be a convincing husband. What other pineapples are you hiding from me?"

She rolls her eyes and collapses onto the bed dramatically. "OMG. I'm so hungry right now."

I glance around the room. "First you're tired, now you're hungry. I'm beginning to understand why we're having problems in our marriage. Where's the room service menu? I'll order you something."

She waves off my suggestion. "Don't bother. Just go have yourself a drink. I'll eat some snacks from the minibar."

Looking at her splayed across the bed is really fucking with my head. Either she knows what she's doing to me and she's being diabolically casual about it, or she is truly oblivious to the effect she has on me.

I swallow hard as I realize I need to get out of this room. "Okay, but you should probably study that brochure. I'll be giving you a test later."

She laughs as she sits up on the bed. "In your dreams, buddy."

I make a hasty exit and head down to the beach bar at the neighboring resort, where you can literally step off the beach and into the bar. When I arrive at the Tiki Torch Lounge, I take a seat on one of the rattan stools and order a Kamikaze bourbon. The bartender informs me they do not stock Kamikaze, so I order a Maker's Mark with a shot of Patrón tequila on the side.

An older gentleman at the bar, wearing a Hawaiian shirt and a white Fedora hat, has a couple of smoking hot ladies in bikinis hanging on his every word as he stares at me. "Try the flaming nipple. They make 'em better here than anywhere else on the island." He holds out his hand for a shake. "Dusty McDonald."

I shake his thickly-calloused hand. "Logan," I reply, leaving off my last name.

"You here on vacation, Logan?" he asks as the lovely brunette in a white bikini traces her finger along the side of his face.

"Something like that," I reply as the bartender slides my drinks in front of me. "Are you a native?"

Dusty smiles as the blonde with the pink bikini whispers in his ear. "Who, me? Nah, I moved here from the mainland about four years ago when I retired."

"Retired, huh?" I reply, trying to ignore the naughty look the blonde is sending my way as the brunette slides her tongue inside Dusty's ear. "What did you used to do?"

I feel like I stepped inside the Playboy mansion. Who the hell is this guy? Hugh Hefner's protégé?

"Oh, a little of this, a little of that," Dusty replies as the brunette slides her hand down the front of his Hawaiian shirt and appears to start pinching his nipple.

Is that what he meant by "try the flaming nipple"?

The bartender shakes his head and walks away to take someone else's order.

I don't ask Dusty what he means by "a little of this, a little of that" for fear that I might not actually want to know.

"So, what do you do and why the hell do you need a vacation?" he asks. "Or are you here on a vacation from the ol' ball and chain?"

"Actually, I'm here on business. I work for my father's investment firm. I'm here doing some…research."

Dusty laughs out loud. "Hawaii is the best place for research," he says, smacking the blonde on the ass.

"You'll pay for that tonight," she murmurs.

"Oh, yeah. What are you gonna do to me, baby?"

The blonde whispers in his ear and a wide smiles spreads across his tanned, leathery face.

Dusty turns his attention back to me. "I made most of my money on the stock market," he begins. "Cashed out right before the big crash of '08 and made a killing. With no wife and kids, I was free to do whatever I wanted. Traveled around for a bit and ended up settling right here in the happiest place on Earth."

Having been born into obscene wealth, I have a pretty good bullshit detector when someone claims to be swimming in cash. But despite his obviously inflated sense of self, I admire the guy for committing to this delusion. At least he seems to have gotten a few things right. No wife and kids, just good drinks, hot women, and a perfect white-sand beach.

I drain my glass of bourbon and throw back the shot of tequila right after. I smack my lips as the heat of the tequila spreads from my mouth outward to my cheeks. The blonde smiles at me as I order a flaming nipple from the bartender.

She turns away from Dusty, taking a step toward me so she can lean in and whisper, "You're a big boy. How tall are you?"

I try not to roll my eyes at this attempt at seduction. "Six-four. And you are?"

She places the tip of her finger on her full bottom lip. "I'm Serafina and that's my sister, Melina," she replies, nodding toward the brunette. "I'll bet you're big all over."

The bartender sets an oversized shot glass in front of me and uses a lighter to set it on fire. I'm thankful for the distraction from Serafina, as my Spidey-sense is tingling. What kind of person names their daughters Melina and Serafina? These girls probably make their rounds at the resorts, looking for gullible tourists to scam.

I wait for the flames shooting out of my shot glass to die down before I pour it down my throat. "You weren't lying. That's a damn good shot."

Serafina seems to pick up on my vibes. "I have to pee," she declares, loudly enough for the elderly couple at the other end of the bar to appear traumatized.

"Me, too. Let's go up to the room," Melina declares, before whispering something in Dusty's ear.

Serafina stops next to me and reaches down the front of her bikini bottoms. She comes up with a hotel room card key, which she slowly tucks inside the breast pocket of my Hawaiian shirt.

"I'm in room 204," she whispers in my ear before grabbing my crotch. "Ooh, see you later, big boy."

As she and Melina walk away, Dusty gets up from his stool, either completely unaware or unashamed that his flag is flying at full-staff. "I'll go up and meet them later. Right now, I gotta take a piss."

I shake my head as I watch him step into the sand and begin walking toward the ocean. As Dusty begins pissing in the crystal-blue water, I spot Kitty standing on beach closer to our resort. She's looking right at me. How long has she been standing there watching me? Did she see Serafina grab my dick?

The bartender says something, and I whip my head around.

"I'm sorry. What did you say?"

"Are you ready to settle your tab? Do you want another drink?"

I shake my head as I hand him my credit card. It feels like he's taking his sweet time as I wait for him to run my card, so I can hurry up and sign the receipt. I want to get out of here so I can catch up with Kitty and find out what she did or didn't see.

But when I sign the receipt and turn around again, Kitty is gone.

Fuck!

Considering where the card was previously stored, I really don't want to touch it, but I need to get rid of it. As I head back to the Hilton Hotel, I reach into my breast pocket to retrieve the card key and toss it in the nearest waste bin. But something doesn't feel right.

I slide my hand back inside my pocket and realize my wedding band is gone. That sneaky little... She used the pretense of slipping the card into my pocket so she could get my ring, which she probably felt against her bare skin when she was leaning in to whisper in my ear.

I dig through the trash in the waste bin to retrieve the card key. I highly doubt it's a valid key, but I can't rule out the possibility. I'm about to set off to the neighboring resort, when I see Kitty watching me from just outside the doors leading to the Hilton elevator lobby.

Double-fuck.

Now, she probably thinks I dug the card key out of the trash because I'm having second thoughts about cheating on Sophie. I would leave the ring and go upstairs if I hadn't decided to use my mother and father's old wedding rings.

It's not as if they're using them anymore. And I knew, since I have my father's hands, that his old wedding band would fit me. I wasn't sure if my mother's rings would fit Sophie, but that worked out better than expected.

I glance at Kitty then back toward the neighboring resort then back to Kitty.

CHAPTER 6

SOPHIE

I'm startled awake at the sound of a soft click. My body floods with panic as I realize someone is trying to break into my house. My eyelids snap open, and I'm reminded that I'm not actually in New York. I'm in a hotel room in Honolulu, and Logan Pierce is sleeping soundly on the sofa. I get a twinge of guilt when I see one leg draped over the arm and the other dangling over the edge with his foot resting on the floor.

But my guilt over his seemingly uncomfortable sleeping arrangement is quickly replaced by panic at the sound of a soft hiss, which is followed by the sound of our hotel room door swinging open. I can't see the door from my vantage point, but the hiss of the pneumatic door closer is unmistakable.

"Who's there?" I shout, pulling the sheet up to cover my bare legs.

Logan groans. "What? Where?"

"Oh, I'm so sorry!" says the same cleaning lady who walked out of our bathroom when we arrived at the room yesterday. And despite being apologetic — again — she continues further into the room and fixes her eyes on Logan, who's still splayed across the sofa. "I'm sorry, Miss. There's no do-not-disturb sign. Would you like me to put for you on the door?"

Logan turns around to face the housekeeper. "I thought I put the do-not-disturb sign on the door when I came in last night."

"It's a simple mistake, honey," I reply, trying to sound like the trusting wife I'm supposed to be. "Yes, please put the sign on the door. We won't be needing any housekeeping service for the rest of the week."

I don't want to worry about hotel staff walking in on anything that could blow our cover.

"So sorry, but if no sign on door, policy is we have to clean," she replies, a faint smile forming on her round face. "If you want no housekeeping, you call front desk. Okay?"

I nod impatiently. "Yes, yes, I understand. Can we be left alone now?"

"Oh, yes, of course. I go now," she says, spinning around and swiftly exiting the room.

I leap out of bed and roll my eyes when I see the

do-not-disturb sign is still hanging on the inside of the door. I quickly crack the door open a few inches and slide the hanger over the lever, then I lean back against the cool mahogany slab to shut the door.

"Do you think she's going to gossip to the other maids about us not sleeping together?" I ask, as Logan rises from the sofa.

His dark hair is messy, but in a way that actually makes me question whether he got up and styled his hair then went back to bed. He's only wearing a pair of gray boxer briefs, and the man has the body of a Roman god: the god of bed hair and pectoral muscles.

This is going to be a long week.

He smiles as he passes me on his way to the bathroom. "Are you afraid they'll find out we don't sleep together and take away your Wedded Warrior amulet?"

My eyes widen as he shuts the bathroom door behind him. "Do you think they'd do that? I mean, if we didn't sleep together, we probably didn't utilize the dildo and the brochure with the tantric sex poses. They might think we're not making an effort."

The toilet flushes and water runs for a couple minutes before Logan emerges smelling like hand soap and toothpaste. "I'd be happy to help you earn your title of Wedded Warrior," he says with a seductive smile.

I push him out of the way so I can get into the

bathroom. "You came in smelling like a brewery last night," I remark before closing the door.

I don't want to question where he went or with whom he drank. It's none of my business, except it kind of is my business. We both have a lot riding on this fake marriage being as believable as possible. If we're outed, my chances of getting Kitty to confide in me are pretty much zilch.

"I'm going to need some coffee before I account for my whereabouts last night," Logan says, reaching for the room service menu as I exit the bathroom.

I shrug as I head straight toward my suitcase to dig out my travel bag with all my makeup and toiletries. "No need. I'm not trying to pin you down. I just want us to be smart about this. We can't blow our cover."

I try to sound as casual as possible despite the fact that inside I'm screaming at myself for feeling jealous of whoever he had drinks with last night. It's totally idiotic. He asked me to go down and have a drink with him. And I'm pretty sure he only left because he was starting to feel some uncontrollable urges. I saw the hungry look in his eyes after I changed into my Yankees T-shirt.

Still, trying to stop myself from feeling something more than friendship for Logan is clearly not working. Somehow, I have to try to convince myself he's off-limits, or I have a feeling I'm going to leave this resort with a broken heart and no byline.

"Are you jealous, honey?" Logan teases me as he hands over the room service menu.

I laugh, perhaps a bit too loudly. *"Pfft!* I don't get jealous. Besides, what do I have to be jealous about? We're not really together."

The smile on his face subsides as he seems to come to a realization he's not sharing with me. "Well, you don't have to worry, pumpkin pie. I may only be your fake husband, but I vow not to fake-cheat on you. Does that make you feel better?"

"Pumpkin pie?" I reply, rolling my eyes as I open the menu and pretend to peruse the breakfast options. "Just do us both a favor and keep your Magnum in your pants, and we'll be fine."

His usual confident smile is still missing in action, and it's starting to make me nervous. "Yes, dear," he replies, reaching for the phone to call in the room service order. "So, what do you want for breakfast?"

I could do with a big slice of Logan pie, but I'll settle for what's on the menu. "Fruit plate and yogurt parfait, please. And lots of coffee."

He stares at me for a moment, but I think he's lost in thought. I have a distinct feeling he's hiding something from me, but I can't let myself get sidetracked by my distrust of Logan Pierce. I need to stay focused on priming Kitty and/or Jason to spew their deepest secrets. Logan is just a tool to help me get a raise. Nothing more.

Logan finishes placing our order, and suddenly that signature cocky grin returns to his gorgeous face. "We can discuss our fake marital problems over breakfast. We need to get our stories straight before we head down for our therapy session with Dr. Mahoe."

I smile as I reach into the top drawer of the nightstand and pull out my leather Moleskine notebook. "I've already written it all down," I say, tapping the leather cover. "I also have the notes in my phone. I'll email them to you, so we can go over them while we eat."

He looks confused as he takes a seat on the edge of the arm of the sofa, so we're facing each other. "Why write it down on paper if you have it on your phone?"

"Because phones can be lost or stolen or damaged. I always copy my notes from my phone to my notebook, so I don't have to worry about losing either one. My phone and my notebook are always kept separate, so I'll always have at least one copy of my notes."

He squints at me as if he's trying to figure something out. "How is it you're still an editorial assistant when you've been working at *Close-Up* for six years and clearly you're their most valuable asset?"

I try not to blush at his compliment. "I think that's

pretty obvious, because of what happened with my boss and the loan."

He leans forward, resting his elbows on his knees. "What happened with your boss? Were you two in love, or something? Why did he do all that stuff for you? I mean, a promotion *and* a loan? Sounds like there's more to that story."

I shake my head. "Is it really that foreign to you that someone could do something nice for someone else without the promise of sex or resorting to blackmail?"

He closes his eyes for a moment looking somewhat embarrassed. "Wow. I didn't realize how rude my questions were until now." He opens his eyes and looks at me straight on. "I'm sorry. I guess I'm just not used to true altruism. I've been conditioned from a very young age to be skeptical of everyone's motives."

I wave off his apology. "No need to apologize. I'm fully aware we come from two different worlds, and yours is a lot more cutthroat than mine."

His expression softens as he looks me over again, but not with the same hunger I've gotten used to seeing. I could be reading too much into it, but I feel like I see a note of pity in his eyes.

"Hey, don't go feeling sorry for me," I insist. "I know I didn't ask for my parents to get sick and die within a decade of each other, but —" I clap my hand over my mouth as I realize I've broken my own rule number four and spilled the beans about my parents. Now, he's really going to start pitying me. "Anyway, what happened with my parents doesn't matter. It's not like I'm on the verge of being homeless. If I lose this job, I have friends who'll help me out."

Shit!

He doesn't seem convinced by my assurance that I'll be fine whether or not this week goes according to plan. But the next words out of his mouth actually ease my mind and make me think maybe, just maybe, I will be okay.

"I won't let that happen," he begins, his resolute tone turning my insides to mush. Then, he holds out his fist to me. "We're a team now. We're in this together. Team Ka'pipi forever, baby."

I can't keep myself from breaking into a smile as I bump my fist against his. "Team Ka'pipi forever."

WHEN WE ARRIVE at Dr. Mahoe's penthouse apartment in the Hilton hotel, I'm surprised to find that she's sectioned off the penthouse into two separate wings. After entering through the mahogany double doors, we're deposited into a foyer with another door ahead of us and one more on our right. The one on the right has a brass plaque etched with Mahoe's name and title.

Entering through the door on the right, we find ourselves in a waiting room. Kitty and Jason are already here, waiting to be called for their ten-minute intake assessment, which happens to be right before ours. A jolt of surprise, and a bit of panic, hits me square in the chest when I see Kitty offer Logan a seething glare, a look so packed with shade I fear Logan may be sucked into her black hole of contempt. Turning to Logan, I'm confused by the way he obviously seems to be avoiding her gaze as he takes a seat on the opposite end of the sofa from Kitty and Jason.

I sit between Logan and Kitty and flash her a smile. "Feels a little like waiting to be called into the principal's office."

Kitty's snarl relaxes. "Yeah, this whole experience is kind of surreal."

Jason seems to tighten his grip on Kitty's hand. If I'm not mistaken, Kitty appears to ever so slightly reject this subtle display of solidarity, stretching her hand a bit to loosen her husband's grip. This is a woman who has been hurt, a woman who is struggling to maintain a sense of self while also attempting to salvage the most important relationship in her life. And despite all the pain and turmoil in her own life, she still makes an effort to heave massive scorn in Logan's direction.

This is not a good sign.

Did she Google Logan? It's not as if she could find out his last name from Dr. Mahoe, because that would be a gross invasion of privacy. While Logan may have a reputation as a massive womanizer in Manhattan society, I don't know if he's dated enough celebrities to be well known outside of New York. Kitty and Jason live in Los Angeles.

Hypothetically, if Kitty did become aware of Logan's reputation, one Google search could show her he's an insufferable man-whore with a penchant for blonde supermodels. Jason is rumored to have cheated on Kitty with a model, though the identity of said model is yet to be leaked, which is why we're here. The difficulty setting on this operation just got turned all the way up.

Logan leans in and whispers in my ear, "You should turn on the voice recorder app on your phone and slip it into Kitty's beach bag, so it will record their session."

I turn to him with mouth agape. "Are you fucking kidding me?" I mouth.

My heart sinks as I consider that Logan's promise not to let me down this week was just part of the role he's playing. I sigh as I realize the lines between fiction and reality are becoming dangerously blurred. I can't start questioning Logan's intentions while trying to pull this off, or I'll never close the deal with Kitty.

I need to keep my head in the game. I can't allow

myself to get lulled into complacency by Logan's promises. And I really, really can't let myself get distracted by these confusing feelings I'm having for him.

I have to operate as if I'm all alone on Team Ka'pipi.

When Kitty and Jason are called into Dr. Mahoe's private office, I turn to Logan and fix him with a hard glare. "I'm going to do this the right way. I'm not going to invade her privacy by eavesdropping on her therapy session," I whisper.

"What about his privacy?" Logan replies, and the question catches me off guard.

I shake my head to clear the jumbled mess his inquiry has created. "You know what I mean."

He smiles. "You think he cheated on her despite the fact that we have no proof?"

I open my mouth to reply, but I stop myself. "I don't want to argue about whether or not Jason is actually guilty of cheating."

"Why not? It's a valid question that you obviously never asked yourself when considering whether or not to come here."

I draw in a deep breath and let it out slowly, giving myself a moment to rethink the words I'm dying to say right now. But it's no use. I have to say it.

"Where were you last night?"

His smile withers. "I told you. I went to the beach

bar at the hotel next door." He watches me for a long moment in total silence, both of us obviously contemplating our next move. "We need to talk about this with Dr. Mahoe."

I chuckle at this suggestion. "We need to stick to the list of fake marital problems we went over this morning over breakfast. Stick to the script."

He rolls his steel-gray eyes as he leans back on the sofa. "Kitty saw me at the bar," he mutters, staring straight ahead, probably so he doesn't have to look me in the eye.

"What did she see?" I ask, keeping my tone casual, though my heart is pounding so hard my chest hurts.

"There was an old geezer there with a couple of girls in bikinis. One of the girls may have tried to come onto me, but I didn't sleep with her."

My stomach tightens into a ball. "Did you do anything else with her? You know, not that I care or anything like that. I just want to know what Kitty may have seen."

He turns his head to face me again. "Look at me, Sophie."

Pressing my lips together, I attempt to steel myself for whatever words may come out of his mouth as I turn my body until I'm facing him. "Just answer the question."

His eyes are locked on mine. "I know you see me as some kind of man-slut, but you should know better than anyone you can't believe everything you read in gossip magazines. And to answer your question, no, I did not do anything with anyone last night. But Kitty could easily have assumed what she saw last night is the reason we're here. And I know you have no reason to believe me, so I'll have to wait for my innocence to be proven. But I don't mind waiting."

I stare off into the distance as a new idea forms in my mind. "This is perfect."

He looks confused. "What's perfect?"

"If Kitty thinks you cheated on me, I can use that as a way to get her to open up."

An enormous grin spreads across his face. "Brilliant, as always."

Hot blood pools in my cheeks. I'm about to thank him for the compliment, when I hear movement coming from inside the office. They must be coming out soon.

"Okay, we have to pretend to be angry with each other," I whisper as the handle on the door begins to turn. "Don't touch me!" I say tersely as I rise from the sofa.

"And you wonder how we got in this mess," Logan replies as he stands up.

I gasp audibly. "You're blaming me for your inability to keep your Magnum in your pants? That's rich!"

Jason and Kitty exit the office and, to my delight, Kitty looks utterly appalled by our fake argument.

Logan addresses Jason. "She calls my wallet Magnum. I'm a shopaholic."

Kitty shakes her head in disgust as she marches toward the door.

Jason raises his eyebrows. "Good luck in there, man," he says, trailing after his wife.

Once we're seated on the sofa across from Dr. Mahoe, I let out a sigh of relief.

Mahoe smiles as she crosses her legs. "You're positively glowing, Sophie. Is that a flush of anger in your cheeks or did you two have a breakthrough while you were in the waiting room?"

"That's just her natural beauty shining through," Logan replies for me.

I roll my eyes. "He's just trying to earn some points because he's a big, fat, lying cheater."

Mahoe's eyebrows shoot up, disappearing beneath her corkscrew curls. "Sophie, I understand your frustration. You mentioned on the intake survey you completed in your online registration that your number one concern is reestablishing trust in your marriage, which you reiterated yesterday at the welcoming ceremony when you demonstrated your amazing axe-throwing skills."

I blow on my fingernails and buff them against my T-shirt. "Thank you. I'm quite proud of that throw."

"You see?" Logan complains, just the way we rehearsed. "She doesn't even acknowledge that I landed my axe on the bull's-eye on the second try. On the *bull's-eye*. She's constantly cutting down my manhood."

Mahoe tilts her head. "How does that accusation make you feel, Sophie?"

I gasp. "It makes me furious! And it's totally not true. I don't cut down his manhood, unless by manhood he's referring to his dirty, stinking lies!"

Dr. Mahoe opens her mouth to speak, but Logan cuts her off.

"Lies?" he replies incredulously.

"Yes, lies! L-I-E-S. Lies. You know, that thing you do every time you open your mouth."

"Name one time I've lied to you?"

I open my mouth to reply, but he cuts me off the same way he cut off Dr. Mahoe.

"And I mean lied to you specifically. Not anyone else, just you. When have I lied to you?"

I swallow hard as I realize he's going off script. My mind scrambles for a way to steer the argument back toward the fake marital problems we discussed this morning, but the fierceness in his eyes is so damn sexy it's muddying my thoughts.

"I'm... I'm not going to get into a he-said-she-said argument with you in front of Dr. Mahoe."

His piercing gray eyes are locked on mine. "I've never lied to you."

I tear my gaze away and face Dr. Mahoe. "Sometimes, when I go to sleep before him, he'll..." I pause as I try to remember what fake breach of trust I'm supposed to bring up here, but my mind is blank. "He'll... Sometimes, he'll..."

"Watch you sleep?" Logan offers, which is not at all what we agreed I should say. "Can you blame me? You're adorable with that pineapple on your head."

I draw in a deep breath. "That's not what I was going to say."

"What were you going to say, Sophie?" Mahoe prods.

"I was going to say...that... Sometimes, he stays up too late watching porn."

Mahoe turns to Logan. "How does this accusation make you feel, Logan?"

He shrugs. "It's true, but it's only because of her rules. She has all these rules that make it forbidden to touch her. But all I want to do is touch her...all day. I can't think of anything else."

What the hell is he doing?

He chuckles. "I mean, come on. Look at her."

Mahoe squints as she tilts her head again. "Tell me more about these rules you have, Sophie."

I flash Logan a peeved look for forcing me to improvise. "I don't know why he's calling them rules. I don't have rules. I have...guidelines. You know, just to keep us from straying from our marriage vows."

"Hmm," Mahoe ponders this for a moment. "Can you be more specific about these guidelines? For instance, do these guidelines determine when and where Logan can be intimate with you?"

I am going to murder him when we leave this office.

"Go ahead, honey," Logan says with a satisfied grin. "Tell her about your rules."

I shrug as my confidence returns. "It's really not a big deal. I don't like public displays of affection, so I've asked him to please stop groping me in public."

"And how does that make you feel, Logan?"

"It makes me frustrated," he replies with ease. "As long as we've been together, she still drives me crazy. I crave her like a junkie craves a fix. I just want her to feel loved and desired."

Oh, man, he is really busting out the charm.

Mahoe nods. "I see. I think I'm starting to get a picture of what's going on here. Unfortunately, this is only a ten-minute intake session, and I have other couples to counsel. I'm going to wrap up this session by asking you both what you hope to get out of this retreat? Sophie?"

I shake my head as I try to come up with something that doesn't make me sound like the prude Logan has made me out to be. "I just want to be able to trust him. I don't... But, you know, once a cheater, always a cheater. I don't know if I can ever trust him."

Logan is silent for a moment before he grabs my hand and gives it a light squeeze. "I just want to earn her trust back. I want to be Team Ka'pipi forever."

Dr. Mahoe smiles. "That's beautiful, Logan."

"Thank you," he says as I wrench my hand from his grasp.

*A*s we're leaving Dr. Mahoe's office, I can feel the hot fury coming off Sophie while we make our way down to the hotel lobby. "Are you going to ignore me all day?"

Sophie stops in the middle of the elevator vestibule, which opens onto the lobby. "Exactly what were you trying to do in there? Are you trying to blow our cover? Because if that's what you're trying to do, that little performance in Dr. Mahoe's office was a great start."

I chuckle, but judging by the raw anger in her hazel eyes, that was the wrong reaction. "I know you had your whole script planned out for that therapy session, but in my line of work — and I am semi-successful in my line of work — I've always found that shooting from the cuff works better than prepared statements when trying to convince someone of your sincerity."

She opens her mouth to respond then closes it again to think quietly for a moment. "Well, next time you want to change up the strategy, a little forewarning would be appreciated. We are supposed to be a team, right? And this little operation we have going on is equivalent to the World Series championship. I think our team needs to stay on the same page. Got it?"

"You're right. There's no I in team. Anyway, that script sucked. I considered just making up some stupid marital problems. Like, my wife is furious at our next-door neighbor who likes to sunbathe naked in her backyard. Personally, I'm on the fence. Then, I realized I'd get a more honest reaction from you if I just said something to piss you off. But that thing about the pineapple is totally true. It's fucking adorable."

She rolls her eyes. "So, what are we doing now? We have, like, three hours before the next activity on the agenda."

I pull my phone out of my pocket to check the time and see I have a text notification. "I have a message from Everett. Let me check this."

I tap the notification and read the first sentence aloud:

· · ·

EVERETT:

Meet me in the hotel bar at 1 PM.

I DON'T READ the second sentence in his message, which reads: We need to discuss the findings from the ethics committee's investigation.

"Why would he want to have lunch with you? Don't you two hate each other?"

"He probably just wants to talk business. We did just buy out a $320 million publishing company, remember?"

Sophie doesn't seem to be paying attention to me anymore. Her eyes are focused on something in the lobby. But when I turn my attention in the same direction, I realize she's looking beyond the lobby, past the glass exit doors, toward the pool, where Kitty is lying on a pool chair lounging with a beverage in hand.

"I have to go talk to her," Sophie declares. "Can you go to this lunch with your brother without me?"

I try not to show my profound relief. "Of course. It's more important that you try to plant the seeds of friendship with Kitty. I wish I could find Jason to do the same, but I really shouldn't pass up the opportunity to babysit my brother. The more I keep him in my sights, the fewer opportunities he has to bribe someone to help him sabotage us."

She shakes her head. "Your screwed-up family almost makes me glad I have no family of my own," she says. "So, I guess I'll see you in a few hours in Dr. Mahoe's penthouse for 'Exploring Tantric Intimacy'?"

"Wouldn't miss it for the world."

I have a strong urge to reach for her to give her a parting kiss. She stands there for a moment as we both seem to be deciding how to part ways. But the moment I decide I'm just going to do it, I'm going to kiss her, she turns on her heel and heads toward the lobby.

Jesus Christ. She must think I'm such a fucking amateur.

I set off toward the hotel bar, which is just off the east end of the lobby. I am anxious to hear what the ethics committee at Angel Investments has decided, but I am not concerned about them finding any fault with my negotiation tactics at Brunswick Publishing.

I've been in contact with Helen Brunswick since our squeaky encounter in the employee break room closet, and she has agreed to corroborate my version of the events. According to Helen and me, the encounter in the closet was a natural progression of a friendship formed over long nights of negotiation and compromise. It had no bearing on her decision to sell her shares of the company to Angel Investments.

When I enter the hotel bar, I spot Lindy sitting at a table near a wall of windows, but Everett is nowhere in sight. As I approach, her face splits into a wide smile.

"Please, don't get up," I give my standard line, so she doesn't attempt to get hands-y with me. "Where is Everett?" I ask, praying the answer will give me an out before I take a seat.

"Have a seat, Logan," she insists. "Everett couldn't be here. He has a conference call with Lugo Investments. They're very interested in investing in *Open Sky*."

"Well, then there really is no point to this meeting, so I'll just be on my way. Enjoy your lunch, Lindy."

"Actually, Everett asked me to deliver the news about the ethics committee's decision for him," she replies smoothly.

A waiter arrives at our table. "Can I get you something to drink, sir?"

I want to tell him that won't be necessary, but my curiosity about the investigation gets the better of me, despite the fact I have every confidence they've found in my favor.

"Yes, please. Can you please bring me a Kamikaze bourbon. Neat."

I take a seat across from Lindy, and the smile plastered on her face gives me the heebie-jeebies. "So, what did the ethics committee come up with?" I ask confidently.

Lindy chuckles as she reaches for her glass of

white wine and takes a sip. "How about you start off by telling me how you got this Sophie woman to agree to be your pretend-wife for an entire week? Did you already sleep with her or is she just that naïve?"

I lean back in my chair and smile. "Wouldn't you love to know? But we're not here to talk about Sophie. So, why don't you tell me what the committee found, and I'll be on my way?"

She purses her thin lips. "I smell another ethics investigation on the horizon, but that is neither here nor there. As you have so tactfully reminded me, we are here to discuss the current investigation. And I am sure you will be very pleased, and not at all surprised, to hear that Helen Brunswick defended you to the bitter end. And the ethics committee has dropped the investigation. Your little deal with Brunswick Publishing is expected to go through after the SEC's enforcement authority has done their due diligence on this acquisition."

"You are right. I am not at all surprised. Though, I am surprised at your apparent disapproval of the ethics committee's findings. I thought we were both on the same side, Lindy?"

She narrows her eyes at me. "You and I haven't been on the same side for years."

The waiter arrives with my bourbon and asks if I would like to order some lunch, but I decline based on Lindy's demeanor.

"Well, I have to say I find your open hostility kind of sexy," I reply, as I realize Everett's absence gives me an opportunity to extract information from Lindy.

She cocks an eyebrow. "I'm not falling for that, Logan. You forget that I learned my lesson with you the hard way, and that's the kind of lesson a girl never forgets."

I guess the claws are out. But I have a feeling I can still make this kitty purr.

"You're certainly right. What I did to you was ungentlemanly, and I don't believe I ever properly apologized. So, let me take the opportunity, now, to say that I was a complete idiot. You deserved better than me, and I'm certain you've found that in Everett. But…"

Her icy-blue eyes are rapt with attention, hanging on my every word. "But what?"

I shake my head and feign a naughty smile, as if I have a dirty secret. "Nothing. It's not important."

"Just spit it out, Logan," she demands.

I chuckle. "It's just that sometimes I wonder what it would have been like if you and I had ended up together. I know it's stupid, but I often think about that time we had sex on top of my father's desk in his study, and Everett and my father walked in on us. Do you ever think about that?"

Her pale face flushes crimson, and she takes a few

gulps of white wine to douse the flames. "I try not to think about that part of my life."

"Really? Because I thought we were pretty good together. I think we could still be good together, you know, if you weren't married to my brother," I reply, leaning forward to encroach upon her personal space. "Speaking of Everett, how are things between you two? I thought you two were solid, so I was very surprised to find you'd attended this retreat in the past. Is my brother treating you well?"

She shrugs, clearly loosening up a bit. "We have our ups and down. You know Everett. He can be a bit of a workaholic."

I shake my head. "Still selling yourself short, Lindy. You're a beautiful woman in her prime. You deserve to be cherished," I say, sliding my hand across the table to grab hers. "You deserve to be worshipped." I hold her gaze for a moment as I softly brush my thumb over the back of her hand. "I just wish that Everett and my father weren't standing in our way, or I would get us a room right now, so I could worship you all...night...long." I let go of her hand and sit back. "Everett and my father have a habit of standing in our way, don't they? They're probably scheming against me as we speak."

I take a sip of my bourbon and wait for Lindy's mind to mull over the implications of my words. I don't enjoy confusing her, but she signed a deal with the devil when she married my brother. And she obviously agreed to help Everett in his attempts to sabotage Sophie and me.

For all I know, Everett's absence at this lunch could be part of a larger plan to distract me. I'm merely trying to get some information that will help me protect Sophie from my brother's schemes.

Lindy glances around the bar before she opens her mouth to speak. "Everett doesn't have a conference call with Lugo Investments today. He already reached an agreement with them this morning. Right now, Everett's on a call with our attorney. They're preparing to have your father's shares transferred to Everett next month."

"Before the December 10th deadline?" I ask and she nods.

I maintain a poker face as I focus on steadying my breathing. It's not as if I didn't expect my brother and father to pull something like this, but I didn't expect it would feel like a knife being slowly plunged into my heart.

Lindy's eyes seem filled with hope. "Maybe we should go somewhere else and talk about this?"

I take a few more slow breaths as I consider my options. "First, I need to know that I can trust you. I need to know this won't get back to Everett. Not yet anyway."

"Of course, it won't."

I shake my head. "I really feel for you, Lindy. You're married to a man who will, most likely, be indicted on racketeering or insider trading charges in the future. You know as well as I do that Everett's taste for bribery is only surpassed by his love of *Star Wars* action figures. But if you help me this week, I promise that you will come out on top, no matter what happens to Everett. And you never know, we may find we like working together. Can I trust you to be on my side, Lindy?"

She narrows her eyes as she ponders my question. "What exactly does being on your side entail?"

"Nothing illegal, as my brother would have you do," I reply smoothly. "If you can get me a copy of all the files for the Sever acquisition from last year, I can put my law degree to good use and look through it, see where you may be vulnerable. Help me protect you, Lindy. Do this for me and I promise, when all this is over, Everett and my father will never get between us again."

Her shoulders slump as she realizes she'll have to wait to get a taste of this Magnum pie. "I'll see what I can do. But in the meantime, how about we reenact that moment on your father's desk. I brought that pineapple-flavored lube you introduced me to. Everett hates it."

I venture a soft smile, though inside I'm grinning from ear to ear. "Oh, look," I say, glancing at my wristwatch. "I'm going to be late for a...couples scuba lesson. I really should get going." I stand up quickly and drop a couple large bills on the table to cover our drinks and a generous tip for the waiter. "Remember, Lindy, all good things come to those who wait."

CHAPTER 8

SOPHIE

I'm about to push my way through the glass doors, when I realize I'm not dressed appropriately to lounge poolside with my new best friend. I spin around and immediately return to our suite, where I change into my yellow bikini. Grabbing a robe off the hook in the bathroom, I wrap it around myself and slip my feet into some flip-flops before I rush back downstairs to the lobby.

As I pass the entrance to the hotel bar, I glance inside to see if I can glimpse Logan and his brother. I am stopped in my tracks at the site of my fake husband sitting at a table with his real sister-in-law, whose name I can't recall at the moment because my heart is suddenly galloping so loudly I can hardly hear my thoughts. Logan is leaned over the table with her hand clasped in his.

Last night, Kitty spotted him having drinks with some bikini babes at the neighboring hotel's beach bar. He claims it was innocent, but now this. Am I supposed to believe this is also innocent? He said he was having lunch with his brother. This proves he's a big, fat liar.

But I already knew that, so why am I so upset?

I take a few deep breaths as I start toward the exit again. I can't allow Logan's inability to tell the truth distract me from what I have to do today. Then again, if he's not being truthful with me about this, it's possible he wasn't being truthful when he promised he would make sure that, no matter what happens at the retreat, I will be taken care of.

I suddenly have a flashback to the moment Brady offered me an advance on my pay. He claimed others in our department had taken payday advances before and that no suspicion would be raised. He promised if the transaction was flagged for review, he would take the full blame.

At the disciplinary review hearing, Brady turned out not to be as valuable to *Close-Up* magazine as he assumed he was. He leveled the blame equally between us, which he claimed he had to do to save both our jobs. I don't doubt Brady's integrity, but living the past couple years with this disciplinary hatchet hanging over my head has wreaked havoc on my stress levels.

Is Logan trying to cozy up to his sister-in-law to undercut his brother's attempts to sabotage us, or is he trying to work both sides the way Brady was?

I head through the glass doors and down the steps to the pool area.

Swiping a piña colada off a waiter's tray on the way there. "Put it on room 1210. Sorry!" I shout my apology at him as I continue toward Kitty.

I take a seat in the padded lounge chair next to her, and I'm about to speak up when the waiter I just stole a drink from arrives. "I said I was sorry. You can put it on room 1210. Is it really that big of a deal?"

The waiter clears his throat and addresses Kitty instead of me. "I'm very sorry, miss, but this woman has stolen your drink. I will bring you another one... on the house."

The waiter flashes me a shit-eating grin then turns on his heel and walks away.

Kitty looks at me in confusion. "What did he just say?" she slurs.

She's drunk. This is already going better than I expected.

"He was just saying that I bought this drink for you," I say, handing her the creamy beverage. "Here you go."

She stares at me dumbfounded for a moment, then she looks at the drink in her hand and her confusion morphs into a lazy, drunk smile. "Thank you. That's so sweet of you," she says, drawing a long pull on the piña colada.

"So, your husband ditched you, too?" I ask, trying not to gawk at the way she guzzles half the drink in one long sip. "Supposedly, some of the guys are getting together to go golfing."

Kitty rolls her eyes as she places her half-empty drink on the table next to her and lies back. "Golfing? *Pfft.*"

"Tell me about it. Last night, Logan went to have a drink by himself," I reply, digging the bottle of sunscreen out of my beach bag.

Kitty's gaze flicks toward me, then she closes her eyes and doesn't reply. She's either wary of my attempt to commiserate with her or she doesn't want to get involved. I have to figure out a way to make her comfortable telling me she saw Logan last night. Then, I'll be one step closer to getting her to spill the beans on Jason.

I continue slathering sunscreen all over my face and body. "Back on the mainland, Logan works long nights at the office, then he'll come home smelling like bourbon...and sex."

Kitty opens her mouth as if she's going to say something, but she decides against it.

"Sometimes, I feel like Logan thinks I'm an idiot. Like, it wasn't even my idea to come here. I know this retreat is his way of trying to make me think he cares more about our marriage than I do, because I supposedly jump to conclusions, and I want to give up at the slightest hint of impropriety."

If there's one thing that cheaters do well it's gaslighting their victims. I've personally only been cheated on once, by a guy I dated in college. He used to cook up elaborate lies about why we couldn't spend a Saturday together. And if I expressed my skepticism, I was made to feel like I was going crazy and overreacting. Of course, I found out, three lonely Saturdays later, he was boffing a barista he met at the campus café.

Kitty opens her eyes and turns her wobbly head slightly so she can look at me straight on. "Logan did something...to break your trust?" she slurs.

"Right?!" I reply enthusiastically. "That's what I keep telling him. I didn't stop trusting him the moment we got married. It's all the little things that pile up, you know, like the late nights and the drinking and the sudden obsession with the gym. It's not just one thing I can point to. It's just women's intuition, I guess. You know what I mean?"

Kitty lies back and closes her eyes again. "I know exactly what you mean. And it was Jason's idea to come here, too."

I tuck my sunscreen back into my beach bag and lie back on my lounge chair. "I am pretty sure Logan slept with someone last night. I just can't prove it. It's not like he smelled like he'd slept with someone. And he came back to the room fairly early. I just have this...feeling. You know?"

Kitty is silent for a long while, and I decide to give her this time to ponder whether or not she should confide what she saw last night. After what feels like an eternity, she finally speaks up. But the thick, garbled words that spill out of her mouth are not at all what I expect.

"I almost envy you," she begins. "I remember the days...the days when I wasn't sure...whether Jason had cheated on me." She lets out a long, wistful sigh. "I kind of miss not knowing."

Her slurred words shake me.

She didn't give me the name of the woman Jason allegedly cheated on her with, but she did confirm that he was unfaithful. I should be jumping for joy now that I'm one step closer to getting my scoop. Instead, her words make me question whether I even *want* to know.

How can I exploit this woman's suffering for my own gain?

This job is so much easier when I'm working in an office, following up on email and phone tips from the comfort of my cubicle. I don't have to pretend to be the idiot who married a womanizer. I don't have to look celebrities in the eye and see them as real people.

I don't know if I can do this for what now seems like a silly promotion and raise.

Letting out a deep sigh, I close my eyes and relax into the lounge chair. It's time to raise my game. I have to take Jen and Gail's advice and flip the switch on Logan. The price of selling my soul just skyrocketed.

"Do you want to have dinner with Logan and me tomorrow night?" I ask, trying to sound as casual as possible. "I feel like this retreat has thrown me off balance. I just want to do something normal for a change."

Without hesitation, Kitty responds, "That sounds nice. Actually, there's a seafood restaurant at the resort next to us... It's — Jason and I have been wanting to try it. But the council meeting is it at eight."

"How does six o'clock sound?"

Her face splits into another drunk grin. "It's a date!"

She holds up her hand for a high-five, but when I bring mine up she moves hers at the last second and we miss. I catch her as she almost rolls off her lounge chair. She apologizes as I help her lie back, and I assure her she's fine. I'll definitely have to remind her about our dinner date when she's sober.

When the waiter comes by with Kitty's complimentary piña colada, I shake my head as he's about to place the drink on the table next to her. He takes one look at her and keeps walking.

With dinner scheduled, the next step in my plan is secured. I now have a bargaining chip to use when I flip the switch on Logan. He doesn't have to know I'm questioning whether I'm capable of violating Kitty's privacy. Besides, dinner with Kitty and Jason may change my mind. She may turn out to be the prima donna she's rumored to be.

CHAPTER 9

*D*espite my accusation that Sophie is disinterested in lovemaking, and her own admission that she doesn't like public displays of affection, Sophie and I are voted Wedded Warriors for the second night in a row. The next activity on the agenda for this afternoon was 'Exploring Tantric Intimacy.'

Sophie has been acting a bit strange since her chat with Kitty. She seems to have upped her game when it comes to convincing the other couples and Dr. Mahoe that she and I are not only married, but very interested in getting the most out of this retreat as possible. During our lesson in Tantric intimacy, which took place in the stiflingly warm and dimly lit yoga studio inside Mahoe's penthouse apartment, Sophie surprised me by asking Dr. Mahoe many in-depth questions about the Tantric massage she was demonstrating on her husband. And when Bobby climaxed, blowing his load like magma shooting out of Mount Kīlauea, Sophie made sure she spoke loud enough for everyone to hear when she leaned closer to me and remarked, "His magma has nothing on your Magnum."

Whatever Kitty and Sophie talked about by the pool seems to have inspired Sophie to refocus her efforts. Either she has a renewed desire to get this scoop, or she's up to something. I'm betting on the latter.

As we enter the suite, I remove the Wedded Warrior amulet from around my neck and toss it onto the room service cart near the TV, which no doubt has our "reward" resting underneath the silver domed lid. I take a seat on the sofa, leaning back as I put my legs on the coffee table. Sophie immediately opens the top drawer of the nightstand next to the bed.

"So, do you want to tell me what that little enthusiastic wife routine was all about?" I ask as she sits down on the bed and begins handwriting some notes in her gossip diary.

She shrugs, her eyes focused on the little red journal in her hands as she continues writing. "Are you trying to imply that you don't want me to be a convincing wife?"

"On the contrary, I wouldn't mind if you tried to

convince me," I reply with a chuckle, but she keeps her eyes trained on her notes.

Her hand stops moving across the page, and she seems to be pondering my comment before she tucks the book back into the drawer and slides it shut. "I know you've been dying to find out what Kitty and I talked about today, but first we need to renegotiate the terms of my compensation package."

The smile on my face stiffens. "Is this a shakedown?"

"Do you mean am I offering you something you desperately want in exchange for something I desperately want? I wonder where I learned that type of behavior, hubby."

I rise from the sofa and head toward the room service cart to uncover our reward. "You've made your point. Let's negotiate," I say as I pop the bottle of champagne and pour us both a glass.

She accepts the drink and straightens her back as she sits cross-legged on the bed. "Okay, I know we negotiated a raise and promotion from my new position as your assistant to travel features editor at *Open Sky*, but I don't think those terms fully reflect the amount of effort and potential backlash from what I'm doing here," she begins, and I say a silent prayer that Everett will not put up a fight when I tell him I've hired a travel features editor for his new magazine.

"Instead of a twenty percent pay bump," Sophie continues, "I want one hundred percent."

I spit out my mouthful of champagne all over her face. "Oh shit! I'm sorry," I say, lifting the edge of the comforter on the bed and attempting to wipe her face. "You want me to double your salary? Oh, shit. I'm really sorry."

She pushes my hands away and uses the comforter to wipe her face on her own. "My salary is $82,000 a year, which is basically starvation wages in Manhattan. Doubling my salary would bring my wages into the 21st century. Unless, you don't think that what I'm doing here is that important."

I set down my glass of champagne on the room service cart and lift the silver domed lid to buy myself some time. Lying on top of a clean white plate is what looks like two event tickets.

I lift them from the plate and read the words aloud. "Come Fly With Me Helicopter Tours. Congratulations on winning your own private helicopter tour of Oahu! Please arrive for your tour promptly at: 11 a.m. November 18th. Please wear sunscreen and water- and wind-resistant clothing. And don't forget your sense of adventure!" I turn to Sophie to see her reaction, but she doesn't seem to have one. "Did you hear what I just said? We won a helicopter tour. Isn't that exciting?"

She continues to appear unamused. "Don't pretend

with me like you don't have your own private helicopter. This is not at all exciting to you. This is an excuse to change the subject, but I will not be deterred. So, are we agreed on doubling my salary?"

"You know, I'm not sure I appreciate this attempt at being a convincing wife. This seems a bit hostile, if I'm being completely honest."

The stony look on her face finally cracks as she lets out a derisive chuckle. "If you think this is hostile, just wait until tomorrow's couples activity: the airing of grievances."

I flinch at her words. "That sounded distinctly like a threat. I'm kind of into it."

"And you still haven't answered my question."

I smile at her persistence, which, if I'm being totally honest, is really fucking sexy. "Okay, if you help me get the scoop that we came here for, yes, I will double your salary in addition to promoting you to travel features editor at *Open Sky*. Happy now?"

She shakes her head. "Oh, I'm just getting started."

I nod along as if this was expected, but I'm actually a bit blindsided. I should demand to know what she talked about with Kitty, but something tells me she wouldn't be making demands unless it was something juicy. She's holding the information for ransom, completely unaware that I no longer need the information. If Lindy is to be believed, I never actually had a chance to win my father's shares.

I set the tickets down on the plate and take a seat on the bed next to her. "Okay, what's your next demand?"

She scoots away from me before she responds. "I want my debt to Kensington wiped."

I pretend to ponder her request for a moment before I reply, "Done."

She cocks a skeptical eyebrow. "Really?"

I shrug. "Sure. Why not? I'll sell my helicopter to pay for your debt. Is that it?"

She stares at me for a long moment. What is going on in that pretty little head? Has she been planning these demands all week, or did she come up with this today after — or during — her conversation with Kitty?

She juts her chin out. "In case our little stunt doesn't work out as intended, I need a glowing — and I mean *glowing* – recommendation letter from Logan Pierce, and—"

I laugh out loud. "There's more? Do you want the keys to my penthouse? My beating heart on a platter?"

She rolls her eyes. "As I was saying, I'll be needing a glowing recommendation letter and two years severance — paid at the escalated rate of $164,000 per year — in the event that our work here does not save *Close-Up* magazine or Kensington Publishing from going under."

My smile quickly vanishes. "Okay, what did I do to you? What is this about?" As soon as I voice these questions, my vision darkens with rage as another possibility races to the forefront of my consciousness. "Did my brother offer you something?"

She lets out a sharp cackle. "Ha! What have I done to give you the impression that I would so easily betray your trust? Could it be that you have a guilty conscience?"

I narrow my eyes at her, trying to pick up on the subtext of her questions. "I don't know, Dr. Bishop. Maybe this is something we can explore more in our next therapy session."

She shakes her head as an expression of utter disgust forms on her face. "Nice save there, Pierce. But I am still waiting for a reply to my last request. Two years severance at the escalated rate and a glowing recommendation letter. What's the verdict?"

"You know, I think you might be in the wrong business. You really should consider working for Angel Investments. Your negotiation skills are, quite frankly, terrifying."

"Answer the question, Pierce."

I take a deep breath and study the hard look in her hazel eyes as I consider whether her list of demands will ever end. "Okay, you'll get your severance package and a recommendation letter should

Kensington Publishing let you go. Satisfied? Want to put away those claws now?"

She slides off the bed and stands up straight so we're eye-level. "Have your lawyer send me the amended agreement, then I'll decide if it's time to put away the claws. Deal?"

I shrug. "You're the boss, apparently."

"I'll take that as a yes," she replies as she starts toward the bathroom.

I take that as my cue to snatch the extra pillow off the bed and toss it onto the sofa as I get ready to turn in for the evening. As she closes the bathroom door behind her, I realize we may be closer to murdering each other than screwing each other. Yet, somehow, this only makes me want her more. I wouldn't mind those claws digging into my back while I ride her long and hard.

This image goes up in smoke when Sophie emerges from the bathroom with her blonde pineapple on her head and a new set of pajamas, which cover her body from neck to ankle.

"What happened to the Yankees shirt?" I ask as she violently yanks back the covers on the bed.

She shrugs as she climbs in and slides between the sheets. "Guess I lost my team spirit," she says, reaching over to turn off the lamp on the nightstand despite the fact I haven't finished getting the sofa ready. "We're having dinner with Jason and Kitty tomorrow. If you get me the revised compensation agreement before dinner, I'm pretty sure I can close the deal with Kitty then."

I should be demanding to know why she's suddenly turned into an ice queen. Or at the very least, I should be trying to melt her icy exterior with my hot magma. Instead, I'm dumbfounded. This woman has thrown me off my game like no woman ever has.

I head to the closet to grab the folded blanket from the shelf. "Good night, Maleficent."

This elicits a stifled laugh. "Good night, Voldemort."

CHAPTER 10

SOPHIE

*O*ur first Tantra yoga lesson takes place in the same yoga studio where Dr. Mahoe and her husband demonstrated how to give a man a fancy hand-job. I was tempted to tell her I learned that in high school, but I kept my mouth shut and pretended to be very eager to try out some Tantric massage on Logan. Now, we're back in the yoga studio to learn sex positions that are supposed to bring Logan and me closer by aligning our chakras.

No amount of chakra-aligning can make me forget that Logan is a self-serving man-whore. Seeing him with Lindy yesterday was a wake-up call. I don't plan on falling under his spell again.

Logan and I return our Wedded Warrior amulets to Dr. Mahoe and claim the yoga mat nearest her and Bobby. As I sit cross-legged near the front edge of the mat, Logan takes a seat behind me, his legs splayed out on either side of me.

He leans forward to whisper in my ear, "If at any time you should feel any discomfort, please let me know and I'll make sure to go harder."

A shiver travels over my skin at his words and the sensation of his hot breath in my ear.

Nope. Not going to fall for it this time.

"Like this?" I reply, then I throw my head back to slam the back of my head into his chin.

"What the—?" he groans, and I can hear the scrape of his hand rubbing his scruff. "I had a feeling you liked it rough, but this is a level of violence I didn't anticipate. I'm into it. I'm the king of playing dirty. Buckle up, baby."

He rises to his feet suddenly, peels off his black Adidas T-shirt, and tosses it behind the elderly couple behind us. Unfortunately, he doesn't toss it hard enough and it lands on the woman's face.

"I'm so sorry, ma'am. I meant to throw it over you," he says as her husband peels the shirt off her head. "I'm really sorry."

I cover my mouth to keep from laughing as the woman looks up at Logan with hearts in her eyes.

The woman shakes her head. "Oh, no, dear. No need to apologize. That's the most action I've gotten in years."

Her husband rolls his eyes at the way she's ogling

Logan. "And she wonders why she doesn't get any action," he says, handing Logan's shirt back to him. "At least you two are trying to work things out now instead of waiting until you're a couple of old farts like us. That's a good sign. You're probably the only couple here who doesn't hate each other."

"I heard that, Sherman," his wife chides him.

Logan laughs as he takes his shirt back and walks to the back of the room to hang it on a coat hook near the entrance, then he returns to take his seat behind me with an enormous grin on his face.

He leans forward again to whisper in my ear, but this time he places his large hand on the back of my head to prevent further injury. "You can play coy all you want, but everyone here can see what is so plainly written all over your face."

"What's that?"

"That you so desperately want my Magnum."

I have to give him points for persistence. If he weren't so gorgeous, and didn't smell so damn good, I'd probably have been on the first flight back to New York last night. The truth is his seductive little comments could absolutely be categorized as sexual harassment, since he is technically my boss. But I think I showed him last night that I'm no one's bitch.

My brain has fully bought into this tough-girl act. I wish I could convince my heart and loins.

When everyone is situated on their mats, Dr.

Mahoe and Bobby sit on the purple yoga mat right in front of us. "Good morning, tribes. I am very excited to show you all a new way to achieve deeper intimacy and balance in your relationship," she begins, flashing a lusty look in Bobby's direction as she straightens her back. "We are going to start out today with the yab-yum pose."

Mahoe and her husband turn to each other, and he bends his knees to support her as she climbs into his lap. "Okay, ladies. Follow my lead and climb into your husband's safe space."

I turn around to face Logan, and I'm not at all surprised to find him wearing a cocky, shit-eating grin, which really complements his dangerously sexy physique. *Holy pectorals!*

He beckons me. "Come to papa."

I roll my eyes as I crawl toward him and climb into his lap. All the other couples are following Dr. Mahoe's lead and embracing each other. The elderly couple behind us even appear to be grinding against each other. Meanwhile, I don't even know what to do with my hands. They're pretty much just balled up into fists, which serve as a barrier between me and Logan's rock-hard pecs.

"Ladies, make sure you lock your ankles behind your husband's back. Gentlemen, if you have back problems, please feel free to move your mat closer to the wall, so you can lean against it for support,"

Mahoe instructs us calmly with her eyes closed as she rests her cheek on Bobby's shoulder, looking totally blissed out.

A soft moan issues from the elderly couple behind us, but I don't dare look to see if it came from the husband or the wife.

I draw in a deep breath, which is laced with the intoxicatingly masculine scent of Logan's warm skin. Oddly, the scent relaxes me, and I find myself lulled into a state of openness. I lift my head a little, tearing my gaze away from his perfect pecs to look up at his perfect face.

"Don't choke on me, Bishop," he says playfully. "Let's show these sex-starved couples how it's done."

I know he's giving me a pep talk to spark my natural competitive instincts, but I don't mind. In fact, I think I'll have a little fun with this.

I flatten my hands against his chest and smile at his barely perceptible intake of breath. I slowly slide my hands upward, my fingertips whispering over the grooves of his muscles. Goose bumps sprout over his skin as I lock my arms around his solid neck and look him directly in the eye.

"I never choke under pressure," I reply in a seductive whisper.

His arms wrap around my waist, and he tightens his hold on me so our bodies are flush against each other. "That's why we make such a great team. Maleficent plus Voldemort forever."

Mahoe straightens her spine as her husband's hands slide from the small of her back to her butt. "Okay, tribes. Now, look into your partner's eyes as you place your hand on their heart. Feel the rhythm of their beating heart against your fingertips. Deep breath in… Deep breath out."

I swallow hard as Logan and I lock eyes. Our right hands land on each other's chests, and his skin is so warm and taut under my fingertips. And the sensation of his hand sinking into the pillowy flesh of my breast makes my skin tingle. I don't know if I'm taking deep breaths, as Mahoe has instructed us to do, because I'm not even sure I'm breathing. All I do know is that the thump of Logan's heart against my hand feels like a call to worship.

"Okay, now lean your foreheads against each other and breathe. If you feel more comfortable, you may close your eyes."

Closing my eyes, I expel a long breath and my shoulders relax as I focus on my other four senses: the scent of Logan's hair, the warmth of his skin, the soft drum of his heart beating, the taste of his lips on mine.

His lips on mine?

Oh, yeah. His lips are definitely on mine.

It's soft at first, a gentle exploration, testing the

waters. But when I don't pull away, when I reciprocate, his kiss turns hungry. His tongue slides into my mouth, curiously seeking mine and a small whimper tumbles from my lips. He nips my bottom lip gently, and a bolt of pleasure pulsates between my legs. I tangle my fingers in his hair, preparing to devour him, when the sound of giggles renders us frozen.

As we pull away from each other, we're both winded as if we just ran a hundred-meter dash. We look around to find a wide variety of expressions staring back at us. Everett looks like a kid on Christmas morning. Everyone else is looking at us with a mixture of amusement and longing. Well, all except Lindy and Kitty.

Kitty looks unimpressed by my public display of affection with the husband who may or may not have cheated on me two days ago. But Lindy... If looks could kill, the look she's giving me probably has the power to travel back in time and kill my mom so I'm never born.

A SLIM JAPANESE man driving a black Jeep Grand Cherokee picks us up at our Waikiki hotel. By the time we arrive at Come Fly With Me helicopter tours heliport, it's pouring rain.

Our driver pulls up into a lot, which is separated

from the heliport by a chain-link fence. "Are you sure you want to do the doors-off helicopter tour?" he asks as Logan hands him a generous tip. "I'm sure they can reschedule your tour for next week if you ask them nicely. The weather is supposed to clear up on Friday."

"We leave the island on Wednesday," Logan replies. "Do you not have any helicopters with doors?"

"Those are all booked today. Sorry."

Logan and I look at each other, then we look through the car window at the torrential downpour, then back to each other. "It's your call, pumpkin pie," he says with a sexy smile.

"Could we not make pumpkin pie a thing?"

"Do you prefer chocolate pudding pie? Or tasty squeeze? Maybe, my little marshmallow?"

I shake my head. "Pumpkin pie will do. And doors-off helicopter ride works for me."

Logan cocks an eyebrow as he reaches for the door handle. "Looks like someone's dying to get wet. You're with the right man. Let's go!"

We race through the opening in the chain-link fence toward the blue helicopter, where a man wearing a headset with a microphone waits for us. By the time we make it inside the back seat of the helicopter, the luscious blonde curls I worked on this morning before yoga class are plastered to my head and face. Of course, Logan somehow manages to look devastatingly handsome when he's soaking wet.

Before I can say anything, the pilot hands us each a similar aviation headset for us to wear. "Do you need to teach us how to use these?" I ask the pilot.

"Nope. You just have to wear 'em. This is solely so I can communicate with you during the tour," he replies, sounding a bit peeved.

I want to ask if he'll be able to hear us, but I don't want to ask stupid questions. As the helicopter charges up, Logan grabs my hands and laces his fingers through mine. This is when I notice he's not wearing his wedding band.

Obviously, we're not really married, so it shouldn't matter if he wears the ring or not. But, now that I think about it, I don't think I've seen him wear it since the day we arrived at the resort.

I shake my head as I realize I don't really know if he's been wearing the ring, and it's possible he just forgot to put it on this morning. I forgot to put mine on before last night's tribal council meeting. But even though I know it shouldn't matter, I can't help but feel like it does. I can't help but feel it's a bad omen, like when I picked team Ka'Pipi out of the bowl at our first council meeting.

As the helicopter takes off, I get a swooping sensation in my belly and tighten my grip on Logan's hand. He gives my hand a light squeeze in return, and the mild calluses on his palm make me curious. What would cause a man like Logan Pierce, a man with access to every luxury he desires, to build calluses?

I let go of his hand and turn it palm-side up to trace my finger along the rough, damp skin. "What are these from? Stroking your Magnum?"

He lets out a deep, resonant laugh. "If you must know, these are from riding Minnie a bit too hard without my gloves on."

I cock an eyebrow. "I sense deception. Are you trying to make me jealous?"

"Are you jealous?"

"That depends. Is Minnie a horse or a whore?"

He laughs again as the pilot banks left and we get sprayed by raindrops forced through the rotor blades. "She's my mom's Thoroughbred," he says, wiping some dampness from my cheek. "My mom doesn't ride her as much anymore, so I'll sometimes offer to run Minnie when the stable hand is out of town."

I feel my chest swell with emotion at this small gesture he's described, which seems in its scope to be sort of like the ultimate first world problem. But it also shows how much he cares for his mother. And this makes me miss my mom so much the ache in my chest makes my eyes water.

As the pilot begins describing the unobstructed bird's eye view of Magic Island on our right, I turn my head to the left to hide my face as I wipe a tear from my cheek. Somehow, without seeing my face, Logan seems to pick up on my overwhelming emotions. He laces his fingers through mine again and lays a tender kiss on my temple.

I sniff loudly as I turn back to him. Every alarm bell in my head is blaring. *He's a womanizer. He only cares about winning You're from two different worlds. You'll get your heart broken.*

He smiles at me as he gives my hand another squeeze. "You okay?"

I gaze into his eyes and, for the first time since we met, the color looks more like a soft-silver than a steel-gray. I smile as I coil my arms around his firm bicep, squeezing tightly as I lay my head on his shoulder.

I'm in a helicopter, flying above one of the most beautiful islands in the world with Logan fucking Pierce. Fuck the alarm bells. And fuck my stupid rules.

"You said you studied journalism in college. Did you always want to be a journalist?" Logan asks, catching me off my guard.

I pause for a moment before a smile pulls at the corners of my mouth. "When I was in college, one of my creative writing teachers asked us to write a short story on the spot and turn it in at the end of class. It had to be a friendship story. She said it could be fiction or memoir. So, I wrote about my childhood best friend, Apple Pie."

"Is this your way of telling me you were overweight as a child?"

I lightly smack his knee. "Apple Pie was the name of the cat my parents adopted when I was a baby. He died a few months before I graduated high school."

"Oh. Okay, carry on."

I let out a wistful sigh. "Anyway, when I got the story back with the teacher's notes, she said my story brought her to tears and inspired her to make friendship stories a regular assignment for all her classes. That was the moment I realized I might actually be able to make a difference in this world. With my words, I could remind people of their own humanity. Of course, once I graduated from college, reality smacked me in the face when I realized the only company that would hire me without any experience in a dwindling print magazine market was *Close-Up*. I hated it at first, but eventually my inner perfectionist kicked in and I decided I would be the best damn staff-writer-slash-research-assistant *Close-Up* had ever seen."

"Then, you applied for the *Open Sky* position and I shot you down."

I look up, and the regret etched in his face makes my heart ache. "I didn't expect to get the job."

"Don't do that."

"Do what?"

His expression is fierce now. "Don't belittle what I did to you, and don't ever discount your talent."

I smile, my insides singing as he places another lingering kiss on my cheek.

As we fly over the one-thousand-foot-high Sacred Falls, our pilot informs us the falls are no longer open to hikers or tourists since the tragic landslide of 1999, which left eight people dead. This is one of the things that makes helicopter tours such a huge attraction for Oahu tourists. The falls can only be seen from above.

"So, this area of the island has basically been untouched for almost twenty years," the pilot concludes.

Logan leans over, sliding the headset aside to expose one of my ears, then he whispers, "I know something else that feels like it's been untouched for almost twenty years."

I laugh. "More like twenty minutes. Put your Magnum away or someone's going to get hurt."

"I thought you liked it rough."

I shrug. "That depends. What's your definition of rough?"

His hand lands on my thigh as he leans in closer, so his lips are brushing against my ear as he speaks. "Your body pressed up against the wall as I tear your clothes off. My teeth sinking into your skin as you cry out for me to fuck you," he growls as his hand slides farther up my thigh. "Your swollen clit aching to be touched, licked, devoured. You'll be begging to have my cock nine inches deep inside your throbbing pussy. And how I'll love to hear you beg."

A hoarse laugh comes through the headset and my face becomes molten hot as I realize the pilot heard every word of that.

"Sorry!" I shout toward the cockpit and the pilot flinches, which only makes me even more embarrassed as I realize that if he heard Logan whispering I definitely didn't need to shout. "I'm sorry," I mutter almost to myself as I cover my face in shame.

"It's okay," the pilot replies with a chuckle. "It's not as bad as the couples who argue during the whole ride."

Once we're back on solid ground at the heliport, Logan tips the pilot well before we head back toward the Jeep to return to the resort. As the SUV winds through highways and city streets, I don't see a single bit of it. I spend the whole ride lying back with my head in Logan's lap as he gazes at me while tracing his fingertips over every feature on my face: the ridge of my brow, the slope of my nose, the swoop of my Cupid's bow, the edge of my bottom lip.

As he brushes some damp hair off my forehead, I close my eyes and smile. For the first time in years, I feel like I don't have to face the world alone. At least, not today.

"Do you mind if I shower first?" I ask as we enter our hotel suite.

"We can shower together," Logan replies without looking up from his phone screen.

While his suggestion is incredibly tempting, it also fills me with panic and shame. Logan is used to dating stunning, long-legged supermodels with perfect skin and luscious locks tumbling over their sharp shoulder blades. I'm five-foot-three with shoulder-length frizzy curls, a smattering of freckles cover my shoulders, the freckles acquired from too many days at the city pool without sunscreen. The scar on my lower-right abdominal area from having my appendix removed is a light-pink, delicately contrasted against my ghost-white skin.

I wear a lot more sunscreen these days.

"I think I can manage on my own," I call back to him, then I shut myself in the bathroom.

Almost immediately, he knocks on the door.

"What?" I call out, using the T-shirt I just peeled off to cover my breasts, despite the fact that I'm alone in the bathroom and I'm wearing a bra.

"I just got the amendment to your compensation agreement from my lawyer. Do you want to look it over?"

My stomach lurches at the mention of the demands

I made last night in a fog of fury. "I'll look at it after I've showered," I reply.

After I've showered, I stand in front of the mirror, contemplating what I should do, now that I realize I forgot to bring clean clothes into the bathroom. A few minutes of agonizing later, I let out a deep sigh and suck it up, emerging from the bathroom with nothing but a large towel wrapped around my body. Without a T-shirt to plop my hair, I've been forced to wrap my head in a regular terry cloth towel.

Logan stands from the couch and stares at me, looking a bit dazed. I quickly head for the closet, where I hung my clean clothes yesterday. As I reach inside to grab the floral maxi dress I brought with me, Logan appears at my side, a dark, animal hunger in his eyes.

"Do you need some help getting dressed?" he asks, tracing the tip of his finger down my neck and over my shoulder.

As was the case during Tantra yoga, being close to Logan somehow relaxes me. I know I should resist temptation and tell him I can dress myself, but part of me wants to be taken care of. This reckless behavior probably stems from losing my mom as a teenager and having to take care of my dad before I lost him, as well. But I'll leave the psychoanalysis to Dr. Mahoe.

I hang the dress back up on the rod and turn toward Logan as I gently tug the towel off my head.

My hair falls out in damp, tangled waves. He smiles as he reaches for the corner of the towel I've tucked in to keep the towel around my body from falling. He raises his eyebrows, asking for permission to remove it without saying a word. My breathing quickens as I nod for him to proceed.

He gently untucks the corner of the towel, shaking his head as it falls into a puddle at my feet, exposing every inch of my naked body. "Holy fuck," he murmurs as his hand reaches forward, landing on my hip. "I've never seen skin so creamy white," he says, tracing the backs of his fingers up the curve of my waist. "So silky soft."

A shudder of pleasure makes my hair stand on end as his hand cups the underside of my breast. "White and soft...like a marshmallow?"

He chuckles as his thumb brushes over my skin, making my nipple stand at attention. "Such perfect, pink nipples." He looks into my eyes with an expression of pure awe. "This is going to sound corny as fuck, but you have the body of a Greek goddess, the ones they painted during the Renaissance and Enlightenment." He shakes his head as he returns his gaze to my breasts. "I'm going to worship this body tonight," he says, gently pinching my nipple, a smile tugging at the corner of his mouth as a soft whimper escapes my mouth.

I reach forward to undo the button and zipper on

his cargo shorts — his tourist outfit as he has been referring to it since we arrived in Honolulu. His hands continue to explore my body, massaging my breasts, pampering my skin with feather-soft strokes over my back and down to my ass. I reach inside his shorts to feel his growing erection through his boxer briefs, and it's more massive than I imagined.

He leans his head back and groans as I move my hand up and down, stroking his rock-hard flesh. "Oh, fucking hell. I hope you know that when I'm done worshipping you, I am going to fuck you senseless."

I chuckle as I slide my hands off his member and underneath his T-shirt to feel those abs I've been unable to stop picturing since he took off his shirt during yoga. And they feel as smooth and firm as his cock. I tug his shirt up, and he takes my cue to yank it off. Taking a moment to admire his body the way he did mine, I smile when I see a shiny skin-colored scar on the right side of his abdomen.

Tracing my finger down the groove between his abdominal muscles, I stop at the waistband of his boxers. As I slowly slide my hand inside, Logan's hands come up to cup my face as he leans in and kisses me deeply. As his tongue dances with mine, stealing the breath from my lungs, I wrap my fingers around his erection. I stroke the length before cupping my hand over the head and lightly tease the sensitive ridge with my thumb. The sticky pre-cum on the tip makes my pussy ache to be filled.

Without warning, he grabs my wrist and pulls it out of his pants, then he quickly scoops me up and carries me to the bed, laying my naked body down gently.

He removes his shorts and boxers before lying next to me. "Before we begin, I want you to know that, you can stop this any time you want," he says, his large hand landing on my belly and sliding up to cup my breast.

"I know," I reply with a nod as his hand begins a slow journey down my abdomen.

"You're certain you want to break rules one and three?" he asks, a devilish smile forming on his lips.

"Right now, I'm ready to break all the rules."

He chuckles softly, but his eyes are still locked on my face, watching my reaction as his hand lands between my legs, covering my mound. I lift my hips toward his hand, the way I did when we were practicing the pelvic tilt pose in Tantra yoga a few hours ago. But this time, there's no clothing between us. It's skin on skin, man on woman, boss on employee.

His finger slides gently over the seam of my swollen flesh, a whispering touch that makes my muscles tighten with anticipation. Tracing the line all the way down past my entrance and back again, he watches me intently as I close my eyes and arch my back slightly. Finally, he slips a finger inside me, and I let forth a small gasp.

He gathers the slickness pooling between my thighs and spreads the natural lubricant to over my puffy lips. When I open my eyes, his gaze is still locked on my face, studying my reaction to his touch. His chest is heaving as he slowly smooths my arousal over my firm clit and massages it tenderly.

He only does this for a few seconds before he slides the same finger inside his mouth to taste me. A slow smiles forms on his gorgeous face. "I'm going to enjoy devouring you."

My mouth drops open as he returns his hand to my pussy and begins stroking me again.

The mild callus on his finger hurts so good. "Oh, God. Don't stop. I'm almost there."

But he does the exact opposite. Removing his hand from between my thighs, he leaves my aching pussy on the bitter edge of satisfaction.

He smiles at the look of dismay on my face. "Don't worry. I won't leave you hanging," he assures me as he lowers his head to lay a soft trail of kisses from my freckled shoulder and up the curve of my neck until his lips are pressed against my ear. "But I said I would worship this body," he murmurs as his hand slides over my belly and past my breasts, stopping to cup my jaw. "And for letting me do as I wish, you'll have an orgasm unlike anything you've ever experienced."

He slips a finger inside my mouth, the same one that was just inside me. "Taste yourself," he commands me. "Do you taste that? Hints of salt and juicy melon."

It's the first time I've tasted myself, and I can't taste anything resembling melon. I swallow hard as I realize this man is a pussy connoisseur. As he leans over to kiss me, my breath catches in my throat and a deep moan reverberates in my mouth.

This is when I say a mental prayer. *God, please don't let me flake out on tonight's dinner with Jason and Kitty. Give me the strength to leave this bed.*

I coil my arms around his sturdy neck as he positions himself between my legs. We make-out like this for a while, skin on skin, the length of his erection pressed against my swollen pussy lips. His hands roam over my body, at times caressing gently other times grabbing greedily. My hands do the same, exploring ever taut muscle, his smooth ass, tracing the tempting V that points toward his gloriously beautiful cock.

He plants soft kisses from my forehead down to my lips, continuing down to each breast, sucking gently on each nipple. I try not to tell him to hurry. I want his mouth on me so badly, but I'm beginning to understand that Logan does not want to rush this.

When his face is between my legs, he looks up at me with a mischievous sparkle in his gray eyes. He plants lingering kisses along the creases where my thighs melt into my pussy. Using just his tongue, he massages the soft layers of skin, everywhere except my swollen bud.

My hips seem to have a mind of their own as they rise off the mattress, attempting to get closer to that talented tongue. Logan takes that as a cue to slide his arms under my thighs, hooking his arms around my legs to steady me as he finally goes for my aching clit.

He alternates between fucking me with his tongue, passionately kissing my clit, and sucking on the tiny, sensitive bump. Never focusing on any one area for too long, he draws out the pleasure for so long, I'm afraid that when I finally do climax, I might pass out. In fact, at one point I become so delirious with lust that I feel as if I'm floating.

Finally, with incredible tenderness, he focuses his efforts on my clit. My entire body, from head to toe, begins to quake violently and uncontrollably, but this does nothing to deter him. The orgasm crashes into me with the force of a freight train. My fingers tangle in his hair as my body folds inward, all my muscles seizing up as I let out a wild moan.

He covers my clit with his mouth, but he doesn't move his lips or tongue. He just stays there until he's certain the category-five orgasm has passed and it's safe to come up for air.

Sliding off the bed, he reaches into the back pocket

of the shorts he removed earlier. He digs a condom out of his wallet, and I smile as he holds it up for me to see: Magnum X-large. He unrolls the condom over his erection and climbs onto the bed, threading his outstretched legs through the triangles of space under my bent knees. Reaching forward, he pulls me up and into his lap. He wants to have sex in the yab-yum pose we learned this morning.

"You can get on your knees, if you want," he murmurs as he wraps his arms around my waist. "So you can control how deep I go."

I shake my head as I take his face in my hands. "I want to do it the way we did it this morning. I want to wrap my legs around you. I know you'll stop if it hurts… I trust you."

The corner of his mouth tugs upward into a careful but proud smile. "I won't hurt you. I…" He's silent for a moment, pondering something, then he plants a tender kiss on my forehead.

I don't know what he was about to say, and the mystery of it evaporates as he carefully slides into me. Using nothing but the strength in his bulging biceps and triceps, he lifts me up and down on his cock, kissing my breasts as he lowers me just a tiny bit farther with each stroke, until he's all the way inside me.

As he leans his forehead against mine, and our

breathing syncs up, I realize I've never felt so full, so utterly complete in my life.

WHEN WE'RE both showered and dressed for our dinner with Kitty and Jason, Logan once again offers to show me the amendment to the compensation agreement his lawyer emailed to him. Now that we've just had mind-blowing sex, the offer almost seems like a form of payment. Like I'm some sort of high-priced prostitute. I know this is not the case, since he offered to show me the agreement before we had sex, so I will myself to push these toxic thoughts from my mind.

I slide my phone into my small Kate Spade clutch and shake my head. "We can go over the agreement after dinner, once I've closed the deal with Kitty."

"Are you sure?" he asks, probably wondering why I'm not asking him to slice open a vein so I can sign the amendment in his blood.

I'm fully aware that not signing it right now removes the incentive to honor the terms of the amendment if he gets the information he needs before I sign. But the fact that he even had the new terms drafted shows trust. He has faith that, even if I sign the agreement, I will still deliver on my end and get the scoop from Kitty. I want him to know that I trust him back.

"I'm positive," I reply casually. "Besides, we have to leave now or we'll be late for dinner."

When we arrive at the Bali Steak and Seafood restaurant in the neighboring resort, Logan and I order a bottle of wine and begin discussing our game plan as we wait for Kitty and Jason to get there. Once our dinner guests arrive, Logan and I are certain I will be able to coax the information out of Kitty once we've had a couple of glasses of wine. All Logan has to do is pretend to flirt with our waitress or ogle a few of the customers.

By the time our dinner plates arrive, all four of us are feeling loose, and it actually warms my heart to see Jason and Kitty laughing together and exchanging brief touches and whispers here and there. Again, I begin to wonder if I can go through with this plan. But just as I'm about to express my doubts to Logan, Everett and Lindy show up with enormous grins on their face.

Kitty – whose had more wine than any of us – gasps. "Oh, my God. Look! It's another couple. Come, sit down. Join us."

Our server scrounges up a couple of extra chairs, and Everett takes the chair next to me, so I'm sandwiched between the two Pierce brothers.

I lean over to whisper in Logan's ear, "Did you know they were coming?"

He shakes his head almost imperceptibly, and the

anger in his eyes as he glares at his brother makes me think he's telling the truth.

Logan and I spend the next thirty minutes attempting to steer the conversation toward safe topics, like our favorite fish and how we like our steak cooked or whether it's supposed to rain tomorrow. But Everett or Lindy keep trying to direct the topic of discussion back to Logan and me. They want to know how our helicopter ride went. Was it romantic? Did it remind us of our honeymoon?

Lindy takes center stage as she begins spewing about how Everett proposed to her and where they got married.

"Where did you guys get married again? I can't remember," Everett remarks as he reaches for his glass of wine.

Logan shakes his head. "You probably don't remember because you couldn't make it. Remember, brother?"

Lindy wags a bony finger at Logan. "No, I'm pretty sure we were there."

Logan insists, "You don't remember our wedding, Lindy, because you couldn't make it."

"No, I'm pretty sure we were there. I remember you sealed your vows with a kiss and the wedding party pulled Super Soakers from behind the altar and started blasting the guests with water guns. It was so cute. So passé and gimmicky, but really cute."

Jason and Kitty laugh. "That really is cute," Kitty beams. "I wish we had done something fun like that. We did a drive-through wedding in Vegas. It was quick, so the honeymoon was way funner than the ceremony."

Lindy and Everett appear defeated, but Lindy recovers quickly. "So, are you two looking forward to the vow renewal ceremony?"

Logan and I turn to each other, completely dumbfounded.

"Oh, you didn't know the retreat ends with a vow renewal ceremony?" Lindy replies, relishing our confusion. "You'll get up in front of everyone and renew your vows. There will even be a justice of the peace to make it official."

"Have you prepared your vows?" Everett asks as he lazily slices into his bloody steak.

"When is the vow renewal?" I ask, attempting to sound casually curious.

"It happens at the tribal council ceremony on the final day of the retreat," Lindy replies.

That must be the activity on the itinerary labeled "Declarations."

I put on my best disappointed face. "Oh, that's unfortunate. We're leaving in the morning on the final day of the retreat. I have something important I need to be back in New York for. But I'm sure we'll get around to renewing our vows sometime soon."

Lindy shakes her head adamantly. "Don't worry about it. I'll talk to Dr. Mahoe, and ask her to move the tribal council meeting earlier in the day, just for you guys."

Kitty is casting suspicious looks in Logan's direction, and it appears to be making him uncomfortable.

Logan takes out his phone and texts me to tell me the women he met at the bar a couple nights ago are heading in our direction.

My stomach tightens as I anticipate my heart is about to be broken. I want to bolt up and race back to the room to avoid the inevitable emotional annihilation.

"Well, hello there, handsome," says the blonde with the obviously fake boobs. "I can't believe you left us hanging. We waited for you to come up to the room all night."

Wait a minute. He *didn't* go up to the room?

Logan introduces the blonde as Serafina, but he can't seem to remember the other girl's name.

"Melina," the brunette replies dryly.

The blonde opens up her pink clutch and digs around inside before she comes up with a gold wedding band. "I thought if I took this thing you'd definitely come up, so you could get it back. Guess you're not so easy, huh?" she says as she lays the ring on the table next to Logan's glass of water. "Hope to see you around again. Toodles."

"It seems old habits die hard," Lindy remarks as we all watch Tweedle-Dee and Tweedle-Dum saunter away.

The ball of anxiety in my stomach relaxes as I realize Logan didn't go up to the room with these women. But as soon as this comforting thought enters my mind, I quickly remember I have to pretend to be angry he even talked to them.

"You didn't tell me you met Melina and Serafina. You only told me about Dusty. And how the hell did they get your wedding ring? Did you take it off?" I ask him pointedly.

Logan lays his hand on my thigh. "They were with Dusty. I didn't think their presence was that important. And the ring was in my pocket for safekeeping. Remember the time I drank too much at poker night with the guys, and I lost the ring in a bad bet?"

Ooh, he's a smooth one. I'm not sure if I should be proud or terrified at how easily he lies.

Kitty rolls her eyes, but it's Jason who adds his two cents. "These things are not always what they seem," he assures me. "And when you're married, you have to give someone the benefit of the doubt."

Kitty cocks an eyebrow. "Well, isn't that such a beautiful sentiment. Here's another revolutionary idea: Maybe marriage vows should be taken seriously."

In the blink of an eye, she grabs her glass of wine and throws it in Jason's face before she storms off. Jason offers a hasty apology, then quickly follows after her.

Logan drains his own wine glass and scoots his chair out. "I have to use the restroom. Will you be okay by yourself?"

"Of course," I reply. "Go ahead."

"Aw, isn't that sweet," Lindy remarks, her eyes following Logan as he heads toward the men's room.

Everett watches the bathroom door close behind Logan before he turns to me with a cocky smile. "I know how charming my brother can be, but you shouldn't get too close to him," he begins, cutting to the chase. "This is what he does best. He charms people to get them to do what he wants, then he moves on. Believe me when I say that whatever you're feeling for him is not reciprocated. And if this whole thing blows up in your face, as I suspect it will, you're going to need a contingency plan. I'm certain I can provide you a better option than anything my brother is offering, because unlike him I will actually follow through."

"I'm not interested," I reply, reaching for my glass of ice water.

"Take some time to think about it. If you care at all

about your future, I suggest you hear me out," he insists as he hands me a business card with a phone number and no name. "My offer is on the back. Don't hesitate to call me."

I turn the card over and my heart nearly stops beating. On the back, he's written a dollar figure: $500,000.

Logan emerges from the restroom, so I quickly stuff the card into my bra.

Everett removes the napkin from his lap and wipes his mouth as Logan sits down again. "Well, that went well. A wonderful meal, Logan. Though, it seems like getting that scoop might be a little more difficult than you anticipated. But – and I mean this from the bottom of my heart – best of luck to both of you," he says, as he and Lindy rise from the table. "For now, I'll look forward to that vow renewal ceremony. Good evening, Sophie."

"Did he try and bribe you during the two minutes I was in the bathroom?" Logan remarks as he cuts into his snapper.

The corner of the business card in my bra pokes against my skin. "No, they were just gloating."

Logan stares at me for a moment as I make no attempt to finish my meal. "Are you okay? Did they insult you or something? Because I won't hesitate to go after them."

I chuckle nervously. "No, I'm just not feeling very well. I think I want to go back to the room."

"Of course. Whatever my ice queen wants, she shall have," he declares with the most gorgeous goofy smile I've ever seen.

After dinner, we arrive at the suite to find our room has been tidied up by housekeeping, which reminds me that I forgot to call the front desk and ask them to put a hold on housekeeping services until after we check out. First things first, I immediately head to the restroom and lower the toilet lid, so I can have a seat as I pull the business card out of my bra and stare at it for a while.

The $500,000 figure is burned into my retinas as I close my eyes and recall how I refused to look at the amendment earlier. Then, I think of Everett's words, his insistence that Logan will dump me once he gets what he wants.

As I stand up and flush the toilet to pretend I used the restroom, my phone vibrates inside my clutch. Pulling it out, I'm surprised to find it's a text message from Dr. Mahoe.

Dr. Mahoe:

I've just spoken with Lindy, and she explained your scheduling conflict. Please rest assured that I have moved the vow renewal ceremony to tomorrow night, which is the evening before your last day at the resort. Good night and good luck, Team Ka'pipi!

I WASH my hands even though I didn't use the toilet, then I head out of the bathroom to show Logan the text message from Dr. Mahoe.

He stares at my phone as I hold it up to face. "It's not like it's official. It's just symbolic. If it were a real wedding, we'd have to get a marriage license. Right?"

I flinch at his words. "What do you mean, 'right?' I don't know how it works. I've never been married. Aren't you supposed to be a lawyer?"

He nods slowly. "Yeah, I'm pretty sure it's totally not official. There's nothing to worry about."

"Pretty sure and totally not are two completely different things. They didn't teach you that in law school?"

He smiles as he coils an arm around my waist and pulls me flush against him. "I studied corporate law. I'll phone a friend tomorrow," he says, leaning in to kiss my neck. "He's a divorce lawyer. He'll know for sure."

I know I should tell him about Everett's attempt to

bribe me. And if I don't tell him, I should definitely not allow him to continue kissing my neck and palming my breast. I definitely shouldn't let him kiss me on the mouth, siphoning the air from my lungs. I shouldn't help him lift my dress over my head, and I really should not let him – *Oh, God* – touch my pussy as if he owns it.

But there's no stopping this runaway train now. The rules were thrown out the window the moment he kissed me in yoga class this morning. And as he lifts me off the ground, so I can wrap my legs around his waist, I know the rules – and I – never stood a chance against this man.

CHAPTER 11

LOGAN

For the first time all week, I awaken in a panic, afraid I slept through our six a.m. wake-up call. But the moment I open my eyes and see Sophie's body inches away from mine, the panic evaporates. After three nights on that torture device the hotel calls a sofa, waking up in an actual bed with this gorgeous creature at my side feels like waking up in heaven. I feel more rested than I have in years.

Sophie is sleeping so peacefully, lying on her belly with her head turned toward me. Silky waves of golden-blonde hair curtain half of her face. She looks just as beautiful with and without her pineapple. I can't help but smile at the way her pouty mouth hangs open, making her appear surprised.

I slide out of bed slowly, determined to take a shower and get dressed without waking her. But the moment my feet hit the carpet, she lets out a soft groan.

I glance over my shoulder and, sure enough, her eyelids flutter open. "I didn't mean to wake you. You can go back to sleep if you want. You don't have to get up for another half hour."

She smiles as she squints at me through the hazy morning light filtering in through the crack in the black-out drapes. "I can't go back to sleep," she mutters as she rolls onto her back. "Today is the wives' spa day. I need to figure out how I'm going to crack the code to get into Kitty's vault of secrets with all those other wives around."

I want to make a joke about getting into Kitty's vault, but all I can think is that I should tell Sophie the truth. I should tell her we no longer need to get the scoop. While we were at dinner last night, I used the excuse of a trip to the restroom to hide the fact I was making a phone call to my lawyer to tell him to make a couple more changes to Sophie's compensation agreement, changes I'm sure she'll be very happy with. But the guilty look on her face, and the smug look on Everett's face, when I returned to the table played to my worst fears.

I don't know for certain that my brother attempted to bribe Sophie in my absence, but I think I know my brother well enough to know that he's boringly predictable. He's a one-trick pony. And if he tried to bribe Sophie, Everett will be disqualified from our little competition. Well, as long as no one finds out I slept with Sophie.

To a certain extent, Everett is correct that money can buy just about everything you want in this world. But Lindsay Lohan proved that money can't buy class, and Sophie has proved to be the epitome of a class act. I hope I'm right that she would tell me if Everett offered her a bribe.

I lie back on the bed so I'm facing her. "You should get Kitty alone in the steam room and ask her in there," I suggest as I lean over to place a kiss on her shoulder.

She chuckles as I turn her onto her back and slide my leg between hers. "I don't know if that's a good idea or a bad idea. Are people more or less likely to tell the truth when they're naked?"

"I plead the fifth," I reply, my erection growing against her hip as my hand slides between her legs. "What are you doing for Thanksgiving?"

She sucks in a sharp breath as I slide my finger inside her. "I don't know. That's, like, two weeks away."

I laugh as I gently feel my way to her engorged clit and her body jerks. "Two weeks is not a long time."

She closes her eyes as her hips buck against my hand. "I... I usually just stay home and watch the

Macy's parade while stuffing my face with mashed potatoes from a box."

I stop as I'm about to lick the pebbled flesh around her nipple, which is when it dawns on me that she has no siblings and both her parents are dead. *Jesus Christ.* How could I forget something so huge?

I remove my hand from between her legs and pull my head back so I can look her in the eye. "I'm sorry. That was an insensitive question."

She smiles as she grabs my hand and puts it back on her pussy. "What's really insensitive is not letting me orgasm," she says, her hazel eyes rolling back in their sockets as she grinds against my hand.

"You don't know how fucking sexy it is to see you using my hand as a sex toy. My Magnum is hard as granite right now."

She lets out a breathy laugh as she continues to use my fingers to manually stimulate herself. "Oh, my God," she gasps, letting go of my hand so I can finish her off.

But my need to taste her the way I did yesterday is overwhelming.

I throw the covers off her, and she squeals as I lift her leg and dive between her thighs. "I want you to spend Thanksgiving with me," I say, parting her lips to expose her spot. "I'll even get you a box of powdered mashed potatoes, if that's what you're into."

She moans as I swirl my tongue around her clit.

"Thanksgiving…with you? Is it really fair to…ah…
ask me while you're…oh, God…"

I suck gently on the tender flesh, unable to control
my smile as her legs begin to quiver. "Not just with
me. With my mom, too," I reply quickly before sliding
my tongue inside her to taste that exquisite flavor I
sampled yesterday.

Her fingers curl around my hair. "Your mom?" she
says, breathless. "That…that sounds serious."

I pinch her clit and gently stroke it as I apply
feather-soft licks with the tip of my tongue. She can
only endure this approach for a few seconds before
her thighs lock onto my head, her back arching
dramatically as the orgasm rolls through her.

"Holy shit!" she gasps as she yanks my hair to pull
me up and on top of her. "Where did you learn that?"

I open my mouth to reply, but she quickly places a
finger over my mouth to stop me.

"Never mind. I don't want to know."

I shake my head and lean in to kiss her. She wraps
her legs around my hips, grinding her slick pussy
against my dick as we kiss. And it's not just any kiss.
It's the kind of kiss you get after you've gone away to
war and returned to your sweetheart years later. It's a
movie-kiss. A kiss to seal fates and topple kingdoms.
The kind of kiss you can only share with someone who
owns you heart and soul.

I'm fucking doomed.

I don't even try to stop so I can grab another condom. I don't want to come up for air. I never want to stop kissing this woman.

But the sound of the hotel room door opening suddenly and violently interrupts us. Sophie gasps as I leap off the bed and reach for the sheet and comforter I tossed onto the floor. I quickly throw the sheet over Sophie's naked body as the housekeeper enters.

The woman's jaw hits the floor as she stares at my erection.

I hastily attempt to cover it up with my hands, but that's not as easy for me as it is for other men.

"I'm so sorry!" the woman proclaims, her hand shooting up to cover her eyes as she turns around. "So sorry. I go now."

Fuck. This is not good.

When I stepped away from the dinner table last night to call my lawyer, Ernest Wilhelm, he confirmed some interesting information for me. After my lunch meeting with Lindy the other day, I immediately asked Ernest to find out if my father was indeed in the process of transferring his shares to Everett. It turns out, as I suspected, that Lindy was feeding me an enormous load of bullshit. She and Everett probably assumed I would slacken my efforts to get the scoop on Kitty and Jason if I believed I never had a chance to win my father's shares.

Of course, that means that Everett probably has

tons of spies positioned all over the resort, people he's bribing to keep an eye on Sophie and me, to make sure I'm not using my dick to get my scoop.

"I will put do not disturb," the housekeeper says as she closes the door behind her.

I sit down on the edge of the mattress and hang my head in my hands as I try to think. Sophie has gone into a state of paranoia every time the housekeeper walked in on us, but I laughed off her concern. I can't believe it never occurred to me that this may have been purposeful. This has to be Everett's doing.

Sophie slides off the bed and sits next to me. "I don't understand why you're so worried about the cleaning lady seeing us having sex. Isn't that what we want her to see? It adds credibility to our fake marriage."

I should tell her about the competition for my father's shares, but I'm suddenly consumed with rage at Everett and Lindy for being complete dirt-bags. But I'm mostly angry at myself for failing Sophie. I had this in the bag and now it's slipping through my fingers again.

At least, if I'm correct that Everett has bribed Sophie or the inept maid, getting caught sleeping with Sophie evens the playing field again. Now, we have to get the scoop.

I should have been honest with Sophie about the deal with my father from the get-go. Then, I wouldn't be stuck with the realization that I'm going to lose the competition and Sophie if I don't get that scoop, because I have to be honest with her at some point.

Unfortunately, it's not in my or Sophie's best interests to come clean to her right now. If I do that, I'll risk destroying any trust I've built up between us. And even if she does understand my reasons for not telling her about the competition, putting that kind of burden on her could throw her off her game with Kitty today.

I'm fucking damned if I do and damned if I don't.

All I can do now is put my faith in Sophie. If she pulls through and gets the scoop, I already have the board of Kensington Publishing agreeing to authorize a ten-million-copy print run on next month's issue of *Close-Up*. Sophie and I will shatter the revenue targets for quarter-four earnings. Even if she decides not to forgive me, the changes I made to her compensation agreement will ensure she walks away with more than enough money to pay off her mortgage and take some time off to find herself.

I heave a deep sigh and turn to Sophie. "I just don't want anything to jeopardize what we've done here. I don't want Everett to accuse me of cheating my way to the top."

She narrows her eyes. "Why would he accuse you of that? You're both working toward the same goal, right? You both want to save Kensington Publishing."

I stare into the hazel eyes I've come to regard with such reverence and lie. "Of course, but if you and I pull out a great fourth quarter for *Close-Up*, I won't encounter any resistance to your promotion or end-of-year bonus."

Her eyebrows scrunch up as she stares off into the distance. "Well, then we have to get that scoop. I'll shower first."

———

WE HEAD down to grab some breakfast in the hotel restaurant before another Tantra yoga class later this morning. In the elevator on the way down, I grab Sophie's hand and bring it to my mouth to place a kiss on her knuckles. She grins and rubs her cheek against my shoulder like a cat rubbing its scent on their possessions.

I seize the opportunity to kiss the top of her head. A strange urge to say three words I've never said to a woman overcomes me, but I manage to stop myself by pressing my lips together and leaning my head back so I can't smell her intoxicating scent. I'm so fucking screwed.

On the way to the restaurant, I'm stopped in my tracks when I see our housekeeper standing near the concierge desk, chatting with Everett.

Sophie doesn't realize I've stopped walking until she's yanked backward. "Hey, what are you doing?"

As if on cue, Sophie follows the direction of my gaze just in time to see Everett handing the housekeeper a thick manila envelope. Both Everett and the housekeeper look in our direction, but the housekeeper at least has the decency to quickly scurry away toward the elevator. Everett waves at Sophie and mimes holding a telephone to his ear as he clearly mouths the words, "Call me."

Sophie's mouth drops open. "Why would Everett want to bribe the cleaning lady?" she asks, though her voice has jumped at least an octave.

"I told you, he'll try to use her to prove I slept with you so you'd help me get the scoop on Kitty," I whisper, looking around the hotel lobby to make sure no other couples are nearby.

She seems to be pondering something significant for a moment before she replies. "You're hiding something from me."

"*I'm* hiding something?" I say, my heart racing at the guilty look on her face. "What did you and Everett talk about yesterday at the restaurant while I stepped away?"

"Is this some kind of test?"

"Answer the question, Bishop."

She lowers her gaze to my chest and shrugs. "I already told you. He was just goading me. You know, making me think he's going to expose us to the other couples."

My gaze burns into her as I wait for her to look me in the eye again, but her eyes keep flitting toward the restaurant and the concierge desk. "Is that really all he said?"

"How about you answer my question first? Why is Everett bribing the cleaning lady?"

Now I'm the one glancing around to make sure no one heard her raise her voice. "We can't talk about this right now," I say, nodding toward the entrance to the restaurant, where the elderly couple who sat behind us in Tantra yoga just walked in. "We have to stay in character for the rest of the day. Tomorrow, we leave this island and go back to the real world, and we'll discuss it then."

She flashes me a look of disgust. "Are you saying this isn't the real world? Everything about this trip is a lie?"

I shake my head as I try to recover from my poor choice of words. "That's not what I said and definitely not what I meant. Let's just hurry up and get the scoop so we can go back and be ourselves again. I mean, not that I'm not being myself now, it's just—"

She yanks her hand out of mine and crosses her arms over her chest. "I'm not doing a single goddamned thing. I'm not going to Tantra yoga. I'm not going to the tribal council meeting. I'm not getting your stupid scoop. I'm not doing anything else until I see the amendment your lawyer drafted."

I draw in a deep breath and let it out slowly. "Before dinner yesterday, you didn't seem to care. Why do you want to see it now? Want to make sure my offer is better than Everett's?"

"I should never have come here with you," she says, shaking her head with utter contempt in her eyes. "I have a spa day to get ready for. Do *not* follow me."

I close my eyes and try to process what a complete shit-storm this trip has turned into. I need a fucking drink. But when I turn away from the hotel restaurant to head in the direction of the bar, I almost slam face-first into Jason Costello, who looks about as happy as I feel right now.

"The husbands' bonding ceremony starts in a couple of hours," he remarks flatly. "I heard we're going on a field trip to a hog farm to kill a pig for roasting, for tonight's vow renewal bullshit."

"Sounds like we have two hours to hopefully drink enough to erase this trip from our memories."

He nods. "Sounds good to me."

CHAPTER 12

SOPHIE

*L*eaving Logan to fend for himself at Tantra yoga, I take the elevator up to our room and grab my little red notebook. The last note I wrote down details our experience at Tantra yoga yesterday morning. I've been trying to keep the notes strictly about Kitty and Jason, but after the amazing kiss I shared with Logan, I wanted to preserve the memory.

I didn't get a chance to write about our dinner with Kitty and Jason. Logan and I both had other things on our mind when we returned to our room last night. Now, with my stomach in knots over the possibility Logan may be hiding something from me, I feel like I don't want to write about what happened at dinner.

I sigh as I plop down onto the bed, which remains

unmade, and begin recording what I can remember about last night. When I arrive at Everett's attempt to bribe me, I consider leaving it out. I shouldn't put incriminating things like that on paper. The last thing I need is for Logan to decide, since he is my boss, he has a right to snoop through my notes.

But I need to preserve my memory of the event. I'm a journalist — okay, a gossip columnist – but I do still like to cling to most journalistic principles of preserving the record for truth and decency. Leaving out important details is lying by omission. Others at *Close-Up* may be okay with this type of deception, but I'm not okay with it.

Well, except when it comes to $500,000 bribes.

This assignment has made me compromise my principles.

I shake my head as I realize I have to tell Logan about the bribe. As soon as I'm back from my spa day with the other wives, I'll text him and tell him we need to talk. Then, I'll come clean.

When I'm finished memorializing my entire account of last night's dinner, I stuff the notebook under a towel in my beach bag. If Logan gets back to the room before I do, I don't want him to find my notes. I want to be able to come clean about the bribe face-to-face.

I change into my bikini and toss an extra change of

clothes in my beach bag to use after my spa day. I consider throwing the only evening dress I packed for the trip, so I can get ready for the vow renewal ceremony at the spa. But I don't know what the locker room situation is at the Mandara Spa, so I'll just have to come back to the room to get ready.

Sliding my phone out of the pocket of my cutoff jean shorts, I see I have a text message from Logan. It's just three words: Here it is. A link underneath the text appears to be a DocuSign link. I get a pang in my chest as I tap the link and it opens up the amendment to my compensation package.

My promotion to travel features editor at *Open Sky* will now come with a raise to $220,000 per year — almost $60,000 more than I asked for. And my severance package, should Kensington Publishing decide to eliminate my position, is $660,000 or three years' wages, whichever is greater.

I sit on the edge of the bed for fear my legs may give out on me. I'm an awful person.

I didn't tell Logan about Everett's bribe because I feared Logan was stringing me along. I didn't want to walk away from this retreat with nothing but a ruined reputation. Everett's bribe was an insurance policy. But now that Logan has proved his sincerity in writing, I can see how he would think I didn't tell him about the bribe because I wanted to wait and see which brother had the better offer.

Last night was the first time since my father's diagnosis that I've actually felt anything more than a superficial connection. And now I've gone and fucked it up. Just like I screwed up when I agreed to that loan from Kensington. Typical Sophie.

I have to make it up to Logan. But *how*?

I shake my head as I realize the obvious answer. I have to get that scoop. I don't like the idea of betraying Kitty's trust or privacy. But if Logan and I don't get this scoop, someone else will.

My empty stomach gurgles, though I don't know if it's because I haven't eaten breakfast or because I'm about to compromise my journalistic integrity.

Tucking my phone into my pocket, I sling my beach bag over my shoulder and leave the suite. On the way to the elevator, I grab a piece of honeydew melon and a slice of bacon off a room service cart next to the suite across the hall. As I wait for the elevator to reach our floor, I place a call to Jen.

"Did you dig up anything good?" I ask her over the sound of Knickknack barking in the background.

"All I found was a production assistant who worked with Kitty on that motorcycle club TV show, the one where Kitty and Jason met," Jen replies as Knickknack's yapping becomes more distant. "She said she's pretty sure Kitty had a miscarriage on set and that's what brought them closer. She said they got married, like, less than two months later. Did you dig anything up?"

The elevator doors open, and I press the button for the seventh floor as I step inside. "Not much. I got an email from a guy who drove them around Chicago last year, while Jason was filming that spy thriller. He said he overheard them arguing, and he's pretty sure they were talking about adopting a child, but it seemed like Kitty didn't want to talk about, so he assumed that meant she was against adopting."

"Oh, shit," Jen replies. "That's pretty big, right?"

I shake my head as the doors open up, and I step out onto the seventh floor. "Not really. I asked him for dates and he seemed kind of sketchy on the details, so I'm not sure I can use him as a source. I'll have to dig a little deeper for someone else who can corroborate his story. Anyway, I have a spa appointment, so I'll have to call you back."

"Wait a minute! You didn't tell me how things are going with Logan. Have you and Mr. Gorgeous consummated your union?"

I swallow hard. "I can't really talk about it right now. I promise I'll call you as soon as I get to the airport tomorrow."

"Okay. I guess I can wait another twenty-four hours, but that's it. You have to put me out of my misery soon, or I swear to God I'll OD on Gail's Twinkies."

"I will. I promise," I reply, ending the call and tucking the phone into my beach bag as I pull open the glass entrance door to the spa.

As I queue up behind a line of guests waiting to be checked in ahead of me, I try to think up some convincing vows to recite at tonight's ceremony. *I promise to worship your Magnum if you promise to keep doing that thing you do with your tongue.* I giggle at this thought and the redhead in front of me glances over her shoulder at me with a stanky sneer on her face. *I vow that from this day forward, it will be Team Ka'pipi forever.* Ugh.

When I finally arrive at the front desk, I'm greeted by a pleasant receptionist with a hibiscus flower tucked into her hair over her right ear.

"Good morning. Welcome to Mandara. Do you have an appointment with us today?" she asks with a warm smile.

"Yes, I'm booked for the Paradise bridal package. My name is Sophie Bishop. I mean, Sophie *Pierce*!"

Her smile widens. "Oh, yes, of course. Please follow Nia," she says, nodding toward the girl standing behind her.

I follow Nia through a heavy teak door into a corridor lined with doors on the left and a relaxing waiting area on the right complete with a babbling tabletop water fountain in the corner.

Nia stops at the first door on the left and opens it

for me. "Please feel free to choose any locker to place your personal belongings. Clean terry cloth robes are hanging inside the all the open lockers. Make sure to turn the lock before removing the key. The keys have flexi-bands to secure them to your wrist comfortably. But if you wish, you can leave your key with Brianna at the front desk, and she will keep it secure for the duration of your visit. If you need to use the restroom, just turn left as you exit the locker room and it will be your first door on the left. Do you have any questions?"

My eyes lock on Kitty, who is in the process of changing into her robe near a locker in the far corner. "Nope. I'm good, thanks," I say, hurrying away to snag the open locker next to my new celeb BFF.

"Hey!" I say when she notices me coming toward her.

Her cheeks flush pink. "Oh, God. I'm so embarrassed about last night. I swear Jason and I are not usually such party-poopers."

I wave off her comment. "Oh, please. I'm just sad you didn't get to finish your meal. Logan sure finished his, if you know what I mean."

Kitty cocks an eyebrow. "I'm sorry. I don't mean to be rude, but...you *really* don't care that those girls were totally flirting with him in front of you?"

I shrug as I step out of my shorts. "I don't know.

What am I supposed to do? It's not like I'm going to find anyone better than Logan."

On the inside, I'm cringing at my own words. Unfortunately, there's no way around this pitiable wife routine. I have to pretend to be as pathetic as Kitty hopes I am, so she can feel better about her own dysfunctional marriage. Only then, will Kitty feel safe enough to give me marital advice or a juicy scoop.

Kitty cringes on the outside. "Eek. Is that really what you think? You think you can't get better than some jerk who basically forgets about you the moment you're out of sight? Nuh-uh. Jason would not be able to get away with something like that."

I pull my tank top off and hang it on a hook inside the locker. "According to Logan, any man as good looking as him — or Jason — is going to be inundated with offers from flirty women. As long as they don't act on those advances, there's no harm in flirting, right?"

"Aw, you poor thing," Lindy simpers as she rounds the corner into our row of lockers. "Is that what Logan has been telling you? That it's good for him to flirt with other women?"

"Right?" Kitty exclaims, high-fiving Lindy. "I can't believe what I'm hearing here. I'm sorry, girl. But you must be drunk on Logan's Ka'pipi if you think it's okay for him to flirt with other women."

This is working so much better than I anticipated. Maybe it's time to go in for the kill.

"Really?" I remark, pulling the bathrobe off the hook inside the locker and hanging my beach bag on the empty hook. "But? How do you stay married if you're never allowed to flirt with anyone else for the rest of your life?"

Kitty laughs as she ties her bathrobe. "Now you sound like Jason," she says, turning the key and removing it from her locker. "I don't have enough time to explain how wrong you are. I don't want to be late for my coconut milk salt rub."

As Kitty walks away, Lindy shakes her head. "Shame. You almost had her. Guess you'll have to try being even more pathetic. I'm sure you'll have no problem doing that. Toodles."

I yank my robe on in a huff. "Bitch," I mutter just as the elderly woman who sat behind us in Tantra yoga yesterday enters my row of lockers stark naked. "Sorry. That wasn't directed at you."

"I've been called worse," she says, using the key dangling from her wrist to open her locker. "Why do you think I'm here?"

I laugh as I shut my locker door and groan when I see the key is missing. Trying the latch, it doesn't open. But, I could swear I chose this locker because it had a key in it.

Shaking my head, I make my way out to the

waiting room to find someone to open my locker, but it's just guests sitting patiently with magazines in hand. I head back toward the door leading out to the reception area.

Sticking my head out of the door, I wave my hand to get Brianna's attention. "Yoo-hoo!"

Brianna's warm smile is MIA. "Yes?"

"I need someone to help me open my locker. I think I may have closed my key inside. I'm so sorry."

She rolls her eyes as she picks up the phone and dials an extension. "I need locker assistance in the female locker room… Yes… Okay, thanks." She turns to me looking distinctly unamused. "Someone should be in to help you in about fifteen minutes."

"But, I'm going to miss my massage. And I have very important…*things* in there. Isn't there someone else who can help me?"

The woman standing at the desk waiting to be helped by Brianna rolls her eyes. "Ma'am, can't you see she's busy?"

I cock an eyebrow. "Excuse me, but I am getting married today!" I proclaim so passionately I've almost convinced myself it's true. "I just need someone to help me get into my locker," I say, stepping out into the reception area as panic begins to set in at the thought of someone opening the locker while I'm getting a massage, and my notebook falling into the wrong hands because this Brianna refuses to help me. "You can go ahead and help this woman. She obviously needs a facial. I'll just use your phone."

Brianna smacks my hand as I reach for the handset. "Stop it!"

"No! Give me the phone," I say as I try to wrestle my arms out of her spindly fingers.

Nia comes out to get the next client and gasps at the struggle going on behind the desk. "What's going on here?"

I immediately stop struggling and step away from Brianna. "Nia! I need your help. You said if I needed anything to just ask. So I'm asking, I'm begging, please can you help me get into my locker?"

"I'm calling security," Brianna declares as she reaches for the phone.

"No!" I shriek. "No, no, no, no, no. Please don't do that. Everything's fine now. Nia's going to help me. Right, Nia?"

Nia seems unsure if she should agree, but she finally nods. "Okay. Show me which locker it is."

I let out a huge sigh of relief and follow Nia back into the locker room, but when we enter the row where I got undressed next to Kitty, I find my locker wide open.

"Is that your locker?" Nia asks.

I chuckle sheepishly. "Guess the latch must have been stuck. Sorry about that. I swear I'm not usually like this. Just wedding jitters. You must see that all time."

Nia rolls her eyes and turns on her heel to leave without another word.

I spin around to face the open locker again, glancing over each shoulder to make sure no one else is around, then I dig my hand into the bottom of my beach bag. Panic rises in my throat as I feel around frantically for anything solid, but all I feel is clothing and my towel. In a state of sheer terror, I turn the bag upside down to dump everything out onto the concrete floor.

My notebook is gone.

It has to be Lindy.

I stuff everything back into my bag and close the locker, leaving it cracked open just a sliver, so I don't lock myself out again. I have to find Lindy. That wily little ginger is going to regret the day she decided to mess with Team Ka'pipi.

I turn on the voice recorder app on my phone, then I slide the phone into the front pocket of my terry robe. Setting off to find Kitty, or Lindy, I turn right at the end of the corridor. The first door I open is a facial room.

"Sorry! Wrong door! Carry on," I say, quietly shutting the door.

The next door I open, I find the elderly gentleman who was sitting behind us in Tantra yoga yesterday getting a massage. He probably was excused from the husband's bonding ritual due to his frailty. I apologize again and hang another right at the end of the hallway. Angels sing as I spot a large wooden door at the end of the corridor bearing a nameplate that reads: steam room.

I race toward the door and yank it open, finding myself in a tiled vestibule where about eight white robes are hanging on wall hooks. On the opposite wall of the ropes, there are two doors, one with a sign that reads "men's sauna" and another that reads "women's sauna."

I begin to remove my robe, when I suddenly remember that my phone is in the pocket, still recording. I decide to keep my robe on, despite warning bells going off inside my head, telling me that I won't survive in a hot steamy sauna while wearing a thick cotton robe for more than a few minutes. Then, I get a brilliant idea.

As I grab a complimentary bath towel off the shelf, I wait for the woman who has just come out of the women's sauna to exit before I take my robe off and wrap my head in the towel. I tuck my phone inside the towel, so the end of the phone where the microphone is located is only slightly obscured by my hair. I puff out my chest with pride at my investigative journalism skills, then I enter the women's sauna.

As expected, Kitty and Lindy are sitting next to

each other, leaning their heads back with their eyes closed. My little red notebook is nowhere in sight. I can only conclude that Lindy has not yet read my notes or brought the notebook to Kitty's attention. I make a point of bumping into Lindy on my way to sit next to Kitty. Both Kitty and Lindy open their eyes, but only Kitty appears pleasantly surprised.

"So Kitty, I was thinking that maybe you could give me some marital advice," I begin. "I mean, I obviously am a total pushover when it comes to Logan. Do you have any tips for how to assert myself?"

Kitty smiles as she sits up straighter. "It's not exactly rocket science. When Jason cheated on me with that little WB slut, I kicked him out of the house immediately. I even changed the locks. When it comes to cheating, he knows I have a zero tolerance policy."

The look on Lindy's face is priceless. She thought she probably had enough time to show Kitty the little red notebook after our spa visit. I can see the wheels turning inside her evil little mind. She had no way of knowing she was going up against the Celebrity Whisperer.

"Zero tolerance policy?" I repeat Kitty's words with genuine curiosity. "So when Jason cheated on you with...the WB slut. I'm sorry, what's her name again? Amanda? Or is it Samantha? I can never rem —"

Before Kitty can confirm the name of the WB slut, Lindy yanks off the towel wrapped around her head, and out falls my little red notebook.

That bitch!

I scramble to attempt to reach the notebook before Lindy, but we manage to get our hands on it at the same time. "That's mine! Give it to me!"

"Don't you think Kitty would want to see it first?" Lindy insists through her grunts.

"Why would Kitty want to read my private diary? Give it back!"

Kitty stands up and, with the deftness of her on-screen biker chick persona, she shoves both me and Lindy aside, so the notebook falls to the floor in front of her. She picks it up and flips it open to a random page.

"Please don't do —" I try to protest, but Kitty cuts me off as she begins to read aloud.

"I spoke with Kitty by the pool today. She seems wary of sharing any intimate details regarding her marriage, but I'm sure the Celebrity Whisperer can get her to talk soon," Kitty reads, then she looks up at me with the most loathsome look I've ever seen. "You're a journalist?"

How could I let this happen? Not only have I compromised my integrity, I failed to see Lindy as a worthy adversary. I never once considered she could outsmart the Celebrity Whisperer. I've been sloppy with my work and careless with Kitty's privacy. Not to mention I lied to Logan about Everett's attempt to bribe me. I'm a bad journalist, a worse friend, and an awful fake wife.

"No, I'm, uh…a gossip columnist," I reply, my shoulders slumping with defeat. "But you should keep reading, the rest of that journal entry says how I didn't want to do this. I was basically extorted into it. I never, ever meant to violate your privacy."

Kitty shakes her head in utter disgust. "No, you just meant to profit from it. I can't believe I actually thought you wanted to be my friend."

She drops the notebook onto the damp floor and leaves the sauna immediately. I retrieve the notebook and hug it against my bare breasts.

Lindy flashes me a shit-eating grin. "You must be so happy you got your scoop *and* you got to sleep with Logan last night," she gloats. "Too bad you had to show your true colors. Now Logan is definitely going to lose the competition."

I blink a few times and shake my head. "What competition?"

Lindy covers her mouth as she giggles. "You really don't know about the competition for Jasper's shares?" she asks, her smile widening at the confused look on my face. "You really did this for a measly $80,000 raise? Wow. You're even more pathetic than I thought. Logan has been playing you. You're not here to play house with Logan so you can earn a raise or get a scoop. You're here to help Logan win majority control of Angel Investments. I hate to be the bearer of bad news, but this sham marriage, this little fling you thought was getting serious, it's all just a game. And you're just a pathetic little pawn."

That sinking feeling in the pit of my stomach, that suspicion that Logan has been keeping something from me, ratchets up to full tilt. The hurt transforms inside me, coiling itself around my heart like a python. I want to cry, but I can't. I won't allow myself to shed a single tear for him, or any other member of the dysfunctional Pierce clan.

I force myself to smile as I slowly pull the towel off my head and reveal the phone I've been concealing is still recording. "I may be a pathetic little pawn, but you're a pathetic excuse for a human being. And I still got my scoop," I say, holding my phone up. "But you will walk away from this retreat with a pencil-dick husband who, judging by the fact this is your second time at this retreat, has never been able to satisfy you the way Logan did. I'll make sure to send you the pink dildo I won this week with my sham marriage once I've finished with it. Toodles!"

"Yeah, well, Everett's offer has been rescinded!" Lindy shouts as I exit the sauna.

I TAKE my time doing my hair and makeup in preparation of tonight's vow renewal. About twenty minutes before Logan is set to return from the husband's bonding trip, I leave the suite and seek refuge in a dark corner of the hotel bar, nursing a single glass of wine as I wait for the eight p.m. ceremony. I want to be clearheaded and at the top of my game when I confront Logan.

At a few minutes past eight, I begin making my way toward the pergola in the recreation area. When I arrive, all the couples are standing in a semi-circle around Dr. Mahoe, a couple of ukulele players performing "White Sandy Beach of Hawaii" by Israel Kamakawiwo'ole, and a man in a Hawaiian shirt and khakis who appears to be holding a Bible. I assume the man is the justice of the peace who will be conducting the vow renewal ceremony.

Dr. Mahoe is explaining the importance of trust. "You have to trust that your partner will be there for you when you need a champion, trust that your partner will share their feelings with you, trust that your partner has your best interests in mind. You have to trust that your partner will fight for you and your marriage."

As I take the steps up into pergola, Lindy and Everett appear intrigued by my presence. Kitty and Jason, on the other hand, are shooting daggers at me through their narrowed eyes. Apparently, Logan is completely unaware of what happened in the sauna today. This doesn't surprise me, considering the brief snippet Kitty read in my notebook said nothing about Logan, and she left the sauna before Lindy and I had our verbal showdown. But the glowing smile and the optimism in his eyes catch me off guard.

I walk slowly through the half circle of couples and take my place next to Logan. Taking slow, deep breaths in through my nose and out through my mouth, I will myself to focus on the script I had planned for today. Then, I look at into his steel-gray eyes and the script is thrown out the window.

"I was worried about you when I didn't see you in the room," Logan says. "But obviously I had nothing to worry about. You are the single most beautiful creature on this planet."

His words stoke the burning fury inside me.

"You want to tell me about your little competition?" I begin.

He scrunches his eyebrows in confusion as he looks around to see if anyone heard me. "What are you talking about?"

I expel a huff of laughter, but I barely lower my voice. "Don't play dumb with me. Lindy told me all about your little competition for your father's shares. What I want to know is when were you planning on telling me that this whole trip...everything you've said to me...everything was part of this sick little game... It was all a lie."

Logan looks sideways in Lindy and Everett's direction and his lip curls up in disgust when he sees the grins on their faces. "Look, I don't know what Everett and Lindy have been telling you, but this was never a game for me."

I lower my voice slightly as the band stops playing and the justice of the peace begins speaking. "Game. Competition. Sham. I don't care what you call it. The truth is you lied to me."

"I never lied to you. I didn't tell you about the competition for my father's shares because I didn't want to put that kind of pressure on you."

I laugh a lot louder this time. "You didn't want to put that kind of pressure on me? But you were perfectly fine basically forcing me to pretend to be married to you to save my job?"

"Excuse me?" the justice of the peace calls out to us. "Can I please have your attention over here?"

Logan and I both roll our eyes as we turn to face the same direction as the other couples. Now that we're no longer looking at each other, the squeezing pain in my chest I felt in the steam room earlier returns with full force. I blink back tears as I take a deep breath and summon the courage to speak from my heart.

"I trusted you," I begin, my voice breaking on the

last syllable. "I believed you when you said you wouldn't hurt me."

"You want to talk about trust?" he replies, a note of anguish buried beneath the anger in his voice. "Everett told me today about the bribe he offered you last night. How many times did I ask you if he had offered you something while we were at dinner last night? And how many times did you refuse to tell me the truth?"

I round on him, no longer attempting to keep my voice down. "I compromised my journalistic integrity for you."

He laughs. "Oh, I'm so sorry. I'm sure you were on a lightning-fast trajectory toward a Pulitzer for your groundbreaking work at *Close-Up*."

"You think what I do is sleazy or unworthy of the great Logan Pierce's respect? Because fucking middle-aged women to get them to sign over their shares is so much more honorable, right?"

"At least when I fuck someone in my line of work, they get the courtesy of an orgasm. When you fuck an unsuspecting celebrity, you just ruin their life. No big deal, right?"

I slide the two rings Logan gave me at the beginning of this trip off my finger and drop them at his feet. "Well, neither you nor Kitty have to worry about me writing anything about you anymore, because I quit! I quit *Close-Up* magazine! I quit this sham marriage! And most of all, I quit *you*, Logan Pierce!" I begin walking away, stopping in the center of the semi-circle. I ignore the slack-jawed stares and the sensation that my heart is breaking into a million pieces as I turn to face Logan again. "I dyed my hair blonde for you."

CHAPTER 13

I'm greeted with a loud chorus of "heys" from Gail, Jen, Brady, and Brady's supermodel girlfriend as I enter the deli around the corner from my house. The smell of cured meats and fresh-baked rye bread envelop me like a warm hug. God, it feels good to be back in New York doing normal things with normal people.

Jen shoots up from her chair and throws her arms around me. "You're alive!" she squeals, and I laugh as she crushes me in her arms. "I thought maybe you'd accidentally packed yourself inside one of those moving boxes. Ooh, you smell like coconut. What is that?"

"It's nothing," I say as I think of the coconut-scented toiletries I stole from the hotel suite before booking myself a flight back to New York without Logan.

My stomach tenses at the thought of him. Mostly because I can't believe how stupid I was to allow myself to get feelings for a known womanizer, but also because there's a small — okay, a *large* part of me is hoping against hope that what we shared during our last night together was real.

I've managed to keep myself from Googling him for the past month, since I gave my little "Brokeback" speech at the vow renewal ceremony. I've busied myself with the sale of my family home and the million trips I took to Goodwill to donate almost everything I own. I kept a few boxes of mementos, photos, awards, and the like. Anything else I couldn't fit in my backpack was sold or given away with the help of Jen and Gail, my rocks.

I place my order at the counter and take my seat at the table. "So, how's the freewheeling life of a freelancer?" I ask Jen, but it's Brady who replies first.

"Getting laid off from *Close-Up* was the best thing that ever happened to me," he says, flashing his girlfriend Elaina an adoring smile. "Working as a freelance editor is so much less stressful. Elaina and I are taking a trip to Greece next month. I haven't taken a vacation in three years."

Jen leans back in her chair. "I totally agree with you. I'm way happier now than I was when I was working for *Close-Up*. No offense, Brady. You know I love you, but that was one toxic hell-hole."

"No offense taken. I didn't realize how much *Close-Up* was holding me back. All the long hours and compromising my principles... And for what? A fat end-of-year bonus? It wasn't worth it."

"At least you *got* a bonus. My last two bonuses were held back to pay down my debt to Kensington," I reply as a girl arrives with my enormous pastrami Reuben.

Gail shakes her head as she immediately steals my pickle, as usual. "It's a lot better now that they're getting rid of the print division," she chimes in with an almost guilty look on her face.

I rub her arm. "Oh, Gail. We're not calling you toxic. We know you'll whip that place into shape now that you've been promoted."

Gail is the only one of us who is not only still working at *Close-Up*, she was promoted to managing editor of the lifestyle section within days of my return to New York. She's tried to get me to chat about what happened in Hawaii, but I don't want to taint her impression of Logan. She claims she hasn't seen him at the office since before we left on our trip. He has since abdicated his editor-in-chief throne to a new guy who, in Gail's words, "looks like he just popped out of his mother's womb yesterday."

Everybody seems to be doing better, except for me.

But that's not for lack of effort. I started a travel blog a few weeks ago, and I've been building up my followers. I hope to grow the blog enough so it will eventually become a steady revenue stream while I continue traveling and freelancing. The income from freelancing and proceeds from the sale of my childhood home should keep me solvent for at least four years while I decide if I want to come back to New York or keep indulging my wanderlust.

"It's too bad everything blew up with you and Logan before you could get that recommendation letter," Gail says. As usual, she's trying to steer the conversation back to Logan.

I shrug as I wipe some Russian dressing off my fingers. "I have another interview in, like, an hour. I've had zero luck on the last eight interviews, so I don't suspect this one will be any different."

Jen and Gail exchange a look as Jen shakes her head. "It would have been really nice to get that recommendation letter," she says, rubbing my back.

"At least they were nice enough to forgive my $30,000 loan. So, now I'm free and clear to do whatever it is I want," I say, trying to remain chipper. "Yep, whatever I want. Like get rejected for one job after another."

Jen wraps her arm around my shoulders and gives me a gentle squeeze. "Don't turn into a jaded old hag yet. The whole mishap with Kitty and Jason will blow over. I have a feeling things will start turning around for you very soon."

I laugh. "Thanks. I'll try to remember not to turn into a jaded old hag."

"Oh, I almost forgot!" Jen declares, as she reaches into her giant tote bag and pulls out the last issue of *Close-Up* magazine, featuring a smiling picture of Kitty and Jason on the cover with the headline: Kitson returns from second honeymoon in good spirits. "You brought America's sweethearts back together. Now, you can go out there and show that big, mean world what you're made of."

"Sure. Right after I finish stuffing my face with delicious meats." I hold my hand up to stop her as she opens her mouth to reply. "No dick jokes, please. I can't spit my food out on my interview outfit."

She mimes pulling a zipper across her lips. "My lips are sealed...around Logan's massive Magnum."

I shove her hard and nearly do a spit-take when she almost falls out of her chair. The rest of our lunch is full of the usual laughter, but it's bittersweet. With the sale of the house closing in a few days, I'll be dropping off the house keys with my realtor and leaving for Japan tomorrow. I'll finally get to release my father's ashes in the same place we released my mother's ashes, the place they met when he was a young ensign in the Navy stationed in Okinawa.

Jen and Gail send me off on my way with bone-crushing hugs, but my body physically aches when I see Gail wiping tears.

"I'll be back here to visit you every few months," I assure her.

"I know. It just feels like I'm sending my kid off to college, and my Petey's only eight. I don't know how I'm going to deal with it when he grows up," she replies as she takes a seat at the table again. "Just go. Go before I turn into a complete blubbering mess."

I kiss the top of her blonde head and kiss Jen on the cheek. "I'm off to my interview. Wish me luck."

"Good luck!" they all bellow as I walk away.

THE SILVER FOX interviewing me for the research editor position with Wired magazine has been asking me about my responsibilities at *Close-Up* for forty minutes straight. I almost want to ask him to please stop wasting my time if he doesn't think I'm qualified for the job. But I continue answering his questions and he continues to regard me with amused bewilderment. Finally, as my interrogation approaches the one-hour mark, I can't take it anymore.

"I'm sorry. I realize this is probably not going to score me any points, but if you're not interested in hiring me for the position, can we just cut to the chase? I have to get home and finish packing. I have an early-morning flight to catch tomorrow."

The silver fox smiles as he opens up the file on his desk and removes a single sheet of paper, sliding it across his glass desk toward me. "Your resume looks great, Sophie. And we received your recommendation letters this morning by email."

I squint at him. "Letters?"

"Yes. I received the letter from Brady Harper, which you sent me, and another from Logan Pierce. That's it right there."

Tentatively, I reach for the sheet of paper he just pushed toward me and begin reading.

To Whom it May Concern:

Sophie Bishop was employed as a Staff Writer and Editorial Assistant at *Close-Up* magazine from 2012 to 2018. During her time at *Close-Up*, Ms. Bishop was responsible for researching and following leads, writing and editing celebrity news updates, fact-checking, and cultivating confidential sources.

Ms. Bishop fulfilled her responsibilities with little supervision and always went above and beyond to maintain journalistic integrity and the privacy of her sources and subjects. Frankly, I've never met a more qualified and principled columnist in all the years I've worked with various publishing companies. Any potential employer would be crazy not to hire her, because no one is as sharp and driven as Sophie Bishop.

I am happy to speak with you or your team should you have any questions about Ms. Bishop's time with *Close-Up* magazine.

Sincerely,

Logan Pierce

Former CEO and Editor-in-Chief, *Close-Up* Magazine

Any potential employer would be crazy not to hire her?

I almost laugh at this break from the formal tone in the rest of the letter, just to make a point. Logan's point being that he was crazy to let me go.

I blink furiously as my eyes begin to water.

The silver fox smiles. "Everything looks good, so we'll definitely be in touch over the next week or so."

"Thanks," I say, standing up. "Do you... Do you

mind if I take this with me?" I ask, holding up the recommendation letter.

"Not at all. That's just a printed copy of an email," he says. "Safe travels, Sophie."

I smile as warmth rises in my chest. "Thank you."

AT A FEW MINUTES past four a.m., I deflate the air mattress I bought to sleep on after I donated my bed last week. Though my flight doesn't leave for another five hours, I know I'm not going to get anymore sleep. I tossed and turned all night, contemplating whether I should call Logan. I don't want to be the type of person who ends up alone because they're too afraid to be vulnerable. But I'm still so hurt.

I know Logan has every right to hold a grudge against me, as well. My refusal to come clean about Everett's bribe was almost as despicable as Logan extorting me to get a juicy scoop. But it's not like there weren't moments when I enjoyed being extorted. Namely, the moments when I didn't feel so alone, like I finally had someone on my side again.

Team Ka'pipi forever.

I sigh as I fold the flat vinyl mattress neatly and place it in the same box it came in. Then, with my heart in my throat, I type an email to Logan.

Hey. I just want to thank you for the recommendation letter. I know you didn't have to do that, especially after the way I left you high and dry without your scoop, but it was very much appreciated. I wish I knew what else to write in this email, but for once I'm speechless. I guess that's no surprise. You probably have that effect on women everywhere you go. I guess I thought I wasn't just another one of those disposable women. Not sure if that makes me naïve or optimistic. Maybe a little of both?

Anyway, thanks for the letter. And I'm really sorry I wasn't honest with you about Everett's bribe. I hope you gave him and Lindy hell after I left.

I'm going to be out of town for a while. Actually, my flight leaves in a few hours. I'm finally taking a trip to Japan to scatter my dad's ashes. I'd like to think that if he were still here, he'd be proud I didn't betray Kitty. And he'd be even more proud I wrote you this email, despite my intense desire to ignore how much we hurt each other.

Take care, Logan.

Yours,

Sophie

––––––––––––––––––––––––––––––––––

IT'S STILL dark outside as I brush my teeth and change into my comfortable travel clothes: gray leggings, soft-pink hoodie, and some slip-on black Converse.

As I make my way to the door with my ultra-light backpack, I stop in the foyer to look around at the now-empty house. In two days, the funds for the sale of this house will be wired into my bank account and this house will officially no longer be mine. All the birthday parties and pizza nights and movie marathons and angsty teenage fights will exist only in my memory. I'll never get to stare at the clock eagerly anticipating when Daddy gets home from work. I'll never get to piss off my mom by eating all the French fries as she's making them.

Growing up sucks balls.

I step outside and lock the front door for the last time. As promised, I ask my Lyft driver to stop by the realtor's office, so I can slide an envelope containing the key into their mail slot. The driver helps me with my backpack, and I make sure to tip him well, then I head inside to the United Airlines check-in counter.

"Hi, I'd like to check my bag," I say, plunking my backpack down on the luggage scale.

"ID, please," the woman replies.

She punches in my information and scrunches up her eyebrows. "Hmm…"

"What… What's the problem?"

She shakes her head. "It seems your gate information has changed. But you should still have plenty of time to make it to the gate before the flight takes off." She prints the boarding pass and hands it to me with my ID. "Enjoy your flight!"

"Thanks," I mutter as I set off to submit myself to TSA scrutiny.

Once I'm through security, I glance at the gate number on my boarding pass, but when I look at the signs above the corridors to the left and right of me, neither of them displays my gate number. I head back toward the security area and ask a TSA agent who's stacking plastic containers onto a dolly if he can point me in the right direction.

He glances at my boarding pass. "That's a long way from here. You should flag down someone on a cart and ask them to take you or you're going to miss your flight."

I sigh as I realize the lady at the check-in counter gave me false hope. "Thank you, sir."

I look down both corridors and, on my left, I see a

guy riding a cart toward me. I jog toward him, flailing my arms in the air.

"I'm sorry, sir. One of the agents just informed me that my gate is very far, and he suggested I get someone to take me there on a cart, so I don't miss my flight. Can you help me out?"

He takes the boarding pass I'm holding out to him and cocks an eyebrow before giving it back. "Yeah, that's not in this terminal. You definitely won't make it there on foot. Hop on."

"Thank you!"

I hold on for dear life as the guy races through the concourse at what seems like a dangerous speed. But I don't question his driving. He's the one who knows how far my gate is, so he knows how fast we need to go to get there.

At the end of the concourse, another man opens a rolling door for us to drive out onto the tarmac. The concrete still bears patches of snow from last week's white Christmas, which I graciously spent with Jen and her family. Pulling my hoodie over my head to stave off the chill, I almost lose my grip on my phone when my driver takes a hard left around a large hangar.

In front of us is a long row of private jet hangars, but only one of the planes has been moved onto the tarmac. And as we draw nearer, my heart leaps into my throat at the words written on the side of the jet: Team Ka'pipi.

As the cart pulls up next to the plane, Logan begins descending the stairs to the tarmac in a viciously sexy navy-blue suit. The morning breeze rustles his hair and he looks like a male supermodel acting in a cologne commercial. I can hear the gritty voice-over in my head: Maybe he's born with it. Maybe it's Eau de Logan.

He smiles as he descends the last step and makes his way toward me. "Did the TSA agents do an anal-cavity search, as I requested?"

I shake my head. "Has there ever been a more romantic opening line?" I ask, my words coming out in steamy clouds.

"Well, I'm not sure how romantic your opening is, but I'm willing to do a cavity search to find out."

I barely hold back my laughter as I watch the guy in the cart drive off. When I turn back, Logan is inches away from me. And in my flats, he looks positively gargantuan, but he still smells divine.

I close my eyes and inhale deeply as he pushes my hoodie back to reveal my messy pineapple. I left it in this morning so I wouldn't have to do it again during my fourteen-hour flight.

"I got your recommendation letter," I say, opening my eyes to meet his gaze. "I take it you got my email?"

He smiles. "I hope my recommendation letter wasn't successful in helping you get a job."

I gasp and lightly smack his chest. "I'm supposed to get a callback this week for a job in San Francisco."

"The position at *Wired*? You don't really want to work with a bunch of tech geeks, do you? Especially when you can spend your time writing about your travels and getting free cavity searches as you traverse the world in your private jet."

I roll my eyes. "*Your* private jet."

He shakes his head. "Actually, it will remain mine so I can write off the maintenance costs, but we have a fleet of jets at Angel Investments. This is my private jet, which is now yours to use as you please. Well, only if you want it. A little birdy told me you plan on doing a lot of traveling for the next few years."

I swallow hard as I ponder his words and how casually he speaks them, as if gifting someone a private jet is something he does every day. "Are you trying to buy me?"

"Absolutely not," he replies with a scandalized look on his gorgeous face. "Unless it's working. Is it?" His expression suddenly becomes serious as he takes both my hands in his, rubbing them to warm me up. "You've been on my mind every second of every day for the last month. And I keep wishing I had been honest with you from the beginning. I wish I had trusted you the way I was asking you to trust me. I was unfair to you. I should have told you about the competition for the shares from the beginning."

"I should have told you about Everett's bribe. I was just...so afraid of losing the best thing to happen to me since my father passed. I was wrong and I betrayed your trust. And to do it after what we shared was reprehensible." I fix him with a fierce stare. "I've never regretted anything more."

His hand comes up and lands on my cheek. "I don't want to have any more regrets. So...I need to be totally honest with you." He takes a deep breath and smiles, but the smile doesn't quite reach his eyes. "For years, it was my job to find the person in a company who was most susceptible to coercion. Someone I could tempt with my charms, my good looks, my sexual prowess to coerce them into selling their company to Angel Investments. If it was a man, I would befriend him, show him my extravagant lifestyle, full of fast cars, sexy women, and more money than you can dream of. If it was a woman, I made her feel sexier and smarter than every other woman in the room. I used people. I manipulated people." The muscle in his jaw twitches as he pauses. "I've never been in this situation, tongue-tied and unable to control everything and everyone around me. But this is what you do to me. And I've come to realize that I really fucking like what you do to me."

I chuckle, wiping a tear as it rolls down my cheek.

"Maybe I don't deserve a second chance," he continues. "Maybe you're better off without me. Maybe you'll tell me to get lost and we'll both leave this airport alone. And maybe someday, we'll even move on and find someone new. Get married and have kids, and maybe it will be even better than anything we could imagine." He smiles again as he reaches up and brushes another tear off my cheek. "But I don't want maybe. I don't want to move on. All I want is you, Sophie. I want you in my bed. I want you in my arms. I want you in my life, because God fucking dammit, you're already in my heart. I can't shake you loose. And even if I could, I wouldn't want to. So, what do you say? Can I fly you around the world and back again?"

I bite my lip to keep from ugly-crying as I nod enthusiastically.

He takes me in his arms and lifts me off the ground as he kisses me. And it's even better than our first kiss, because this time it's playful and passionate, packed with emotion and history, or as Dr. Mahoe might say, *true intimacy*. As I pull away, he leans his forehead against mine and we breathe together for a moment before he puts me back down on the tarmac.

I shake my head as I try to regain my composure. "So, what happened with the competition? Did Everett win your father's shares?"

"My dad decided not to retire. I believe his exact

words were, 'I'll have to put off retirement until you two can learn to act like adults. At this rate, I'd have more fun passing a kidney stone than passing my legacy down to either of you.'"

"Oof. That's harsh," I say, though I can't help but laugh.

He chuckles with me. "That's good ol' Jasper Pierce for you. So, what do you say, pumpkin pie? Want to give this thing a spin? Maybe take a two-day layover in Okinawa followed by a short hop to Tokyo for the New Year?"

I lean into the warmth of his palm. "Sounds like a plan."

He kisses my forehead and pulls me into his arms. Burying my face in his blazer, I breathe in that intoxicatingly masculine scent. And at the same time, I can hear him inhaling the scent of my pineapple. We stand like this for a while, completely oblivious of the bitter morning air, until I reluctantly loosen my hold on him.

"I could have probably stayed like that for the rest of my life," he laments, leaning in to kiss the tip of my cold nose. "But I guess it's better if we do that inside the plane, where it's nice and warm. You know, it's better to do cavity searches in a warm, relaxed environment."

I roll my eyes. "If you mention cavity searches one

more time, I might just learn to fly this thing and use it to run you over."

"Well, you clearly don't understand how planes work, because it's really hard to run someone over when you're flying 30,000 feet above the earth. But, I will say I'm glad I decided to give you a plane instead of my original idea, which was to get you a hatchet. You know, to break down the barriers to *true intimacy*."

I shake my head. "I don't think we'll ever forget the lessons we learned from Dr. Mahoe."

"I should hope not," he replies, then he leans in, his lips brushing my ears as he murmurs, "I love you, Maleficent."

I smile as I whisper, "I love you, Voldemort."

EPILOGUE

SOPHIE

The sound of twenty-month-old Caden's laughter is like music to my ears. But the sight of him running around on the lush green grass, in the same backyard where my dad used to practice volleyball with me when I was in middle school, gives me goose bumps. I don't know if I'll ever be able to repay Logan for swooping in with an exorbitant cash offer to buy out the person who purchased my childhood home three years ago. But getting to spend my thirtieth birthday here is more than I ever could have hoped for.

It's true that money can't buy love, but it sure works for making grand gestures. And Logan is the king of grand gestures. My king.

As Logan chases after Caden, and our boy bellows with hiccuping laughter, Jen comes out onto the patio with three glasses of iced tea. She sets the beverages on the patio table and sinks into the cushioned chair next to me. Gail and her husband follow closely behind her, her husband carrying two drinks while Gail brings out the birthday cake she baked for me.

Jen kicks up her legs and rests her feet on my lap as she stares at her phone. "Too bad Brady couldn't be here. He's in Egypt now," she says, turning the screen toward me so I can see the picture of Brady and his wife posing in front of a pyramid.

"Maybe I should ask him to bring back a mummy for his orphaned ex-employee. You know, as a birthday gift," I reply, reaching for my glass of iced tea.

Logan finally swoops up Caden in his arms and heads toward us. "Did you tell them?" he asks as he takes the seat next to me with our son in his lap.

"Tell us what?" Gail inquires as she begins sticking thirty candles in the top of the chocolate cake.

I glance around the table at the eager faces staring back at me, and I can't control my stupid grin. "Jasper just announced that Logan will be his successor after he retires next year."

Jen gasps, removing her feet from my lap as she sits up straight. "I knew it! You owe me a hundred dollars," she reminds me.

Logan narrows his eyes at me. "You bet against me?"

I shrug. "Someone had to. It's not a bet if everyone

makes the same prediction," I say, grabbing Caden as he reaches for me. "We all knew you'd win."

"I always win," he replies, a look of pure adoration in his eyes as he stands up and leans over to plant a kiss on my temple. "Which reminds me, I have your birthday gift."

"Ooh, what is it?" I ask, grinning as he walks away. "Is it a new pink dildo?"

"Dildo," Caden repeats.

Logan laughs and shakes his head as he enters the house through the back door.

I brush Caden's golden-brown hair out of his face and look into silver eyes. "Mommy said 'pink dodo' like a dodo bird. Can you say dodo? Dodo," I say, stretching out the vowels.

"Dodo," he repeats as he reaches for my necklace. "Mommy dodo."

Jen laughs. "That kid is so good at knowing which words go together. You may have the next Hemingway right there."

I pry my necklace out of Caden's chubby fingers and pull him into a tight hug. "I don't know about the next Hemingway," I say, my heart melting as he tucks his hands into the space between his belly and my chest, then rests his round head on my shoulder. "More like the next Banksy. You should see what he did to the walls in his playroom yesterday."

"I'm sorry, Mommy," he mutters.

I squeeze him tightly again. "It's okay, baby. We all get the urge to stick it to the man every now and then. Mommy still loves you," I say, planting a kiss on the top of his head.

Logan emerges from the back door with one hand behind his back and a mischievous smile on his face as he walks toward me. "Close your eyes."

I loosen my hold on Caden and turn him around on my lap, so he's facing his father. "This is my human shield, so you can't surprise me with a pie in the face. Activate your force field, Cadet Caden."

He puts his hands together in front of his chest, like he's praying, and shouts, "Force field!"

Logan shakes his head. "You can only use that so many times before I figure out a way to bypass the force field."

"Never! You'll never get through. Right, Cadet?" I declare, relishing the sound of his laughter as I tickle Caden.

Logan kneels down next to me, smiling as he waits patiently for us to stop laughing. "Close your eyes, Mommy."

"Okay, okay," I say, closing my eyes as I pull Caden toward me so he doesn't slip off my lap. "Okay, I'm ready."

The sound of Jen and Gail gasping almost makes me open my eyes, but I squeeze them shut to stop myself.

"What are you doing?" I plead. "The suspense is killing me."

He laughs, but through his laughter I hear the sound of footsteps. "Okay, open your eyes."

I open them and a large lump forms in my throat at the sight before me. Standing all around the patio table are Logan's parents and all the couples from the Paradise Tantra retreat, where Logan and I began our crazy love story. Even Everett and Lindy, Kitty and Jason, and Dr. Mahoe and Bobby are there. Gail takes Caden from me as I cover my mouth in utter shock.

"Surprise!" they all shout in unison.

"Oh, my God," I whisper as I look around at all the smiling faces.

Logan grabs my hand and I gasp as I realize he's still kneeling down in front of me. "I know when we got married two and a half years ago, you insisted we do a courthouse ceremony, because you couldn't bear the idea of having a big wedding without your parents. And I obliged, because there's nothing I wouldn't do for you. But I figured for your thirtieth, we could do a proper vow renewal ceremony in the presence of all the people who should have been there the first time." He opens the ring box in his hand and tears stream down my face as I recognize his mother's ring, the same ring I wore while pretending to be his wife. "Sophie Pierce, love of my life and royal pain in my ass. Maleficent to my Voldemort. My favorite member of the Ka'pipi tribe. Will you marry me...again?"

I throw myself at him as I pull him into a bone-crushing embrace. "Yes!" I blubber. "I'd marry you a thousand times."

He laughs as he pulls away so he can put the ring on my finger. "I love you, Soph."

I smile as I wipe tears from my face. "I love you."

With incredible ease, which indicates a lot of planning, Jen and Gail set up chairs in the backyard for the guests to sit down as Logan and I renew our vows in the backyard of my childhood home. I'm unable to hide my overwhelming emotions as I recite the vows I'm forced to make up on the spot, in front of all my friends, old and new, including the same justice of the peace who watched me rip Logan apart in Hawaii. And when it's all over, I kiss Logan like my life depends on it.

"Happy birthday, pumpkin pie," he murmurs as he rests his forehead against mine.

"I've never felt so complete," I say, placing my hand over his chest to feel his heart beating against my fingertips. "Thank you for knowing how much I needed this."

He kisses the tip of my nose. "Team Ka'pipi forever?"

I nod. "Forever and ever."

The End.

More love stories to lose yourself in at cassialeo.com/books/. Or turn the page for a free preview of *Break*, a stand-alone enemies-to-lovers romance!

CHARLEY

Then

They say a picture is worth a thousand words. I would say a picture is worth a lifetime of words, since a single photograph can change your entire life.

When I was fourteen, a chubby girl in my freshman Spanish class attempted suicide after her former boyfriend posted a naked photo of her on MySpace. It was the scandal of the school year. I publicly expressed my disappointment with the way my fellow classmates were body-shaming her. Privately, though, I judged that girl. I couldn't help but wonder... Who would be foolish enough to trust a teenage boy with nudes?

Just ten more minutes. Don't pass out yet. Just hold on for ten more minutes.

I repeat the words over and over in my mind, like a mantra. Just ten more minutes and I can go home, drink a gallon of NyQuil, and sleep away this dreadful flu.

The art gallery just off the Sonoma State campus is

small, but not quaint. Situated in the middle of 4th Street in Santa Rosa, among an eclectic mix of upscale and fair trade shops, the gallery has a wall of windows facing south. This wouldn't be a problem if it wasn't eighty-two degrees outside and the gallery's air conditioning wasn't working.

I loosen my black scarf and swallow the saliva pooling in my mouth as the urge to vomit begins to overtake me again. Closing my eyes, I take a few deep breaths as I attempt to quell the sensation.

"I'm sorry. I just need a minute," I say to my professor as we move onto the next photograph in the exhibit.

If I knew, when I chose to be an art major, that I'd have to do my final exam — a solo show using selected pieces from my photography portfolio to tell a story — in an overheated art gallery, while secretly popping Tylenol every time my professor turns his back on me, I might have seriously reconsidered my dream of being the next Annie Leibovitz. Or I might have chosen a major where I could take my final exam in an air-conditioned lecture hall. At the very least, I'd rethink my brilliant idea to wear a scarf today.

My attempt to look like an artsy-fartsy ballerina — in my lucky black scarf, baby-pink bateau-neck top, black skinny jeans, and pink ballerina flats — and my refusal to request a postponement of the solo show the moment I came down with the flu, will be my downfall. No matter how hot it gets in this gallery, I *can't* take off my lucky scarf. Therefore, I predict, if I don't get high marks on this final, I'm going to drop dead on the high-gloss marble floor.

I trail behind Professor Healy like a baby duckling, answering his questions about lenses, exposures, and filters while trying not to stare at the Florida-shaped birthmark in the center of his bald spot. The show is supposed to tell a story, and the only story that matters in my world is the story of Ben and me. The exhibit begins with images of the beach, where Ben and I first met, then moves through a collection of places we've visited together. With Ben's fame becoming such an issue these past few years, most of the pictures depict secluded landscapes: sparkling lakes, rocky coves, and misty forests.

As I discreetly wipe the sweat trickling down the back of my ear, my phone vibrates in my hand. I quickly slide it into my back pocket as we approach the picture I took of the Sky-house.

The Sky-house is a hollowed out Redwood tree near the forested campsites of the Bodega sand dunes, just steps away from where my boyfriend Ben Hayes and I grew up next door to each other in Bodega Bay, California. The Sky-house was Ben's hideout before it became ours, and we promised we would never reveal the location to anyone. He approves of my use of the photo for my final, but I'm supposed to destroy the evidence after my solo show. We named our tree the Sky-house because you can look straight up through the hollow trunk and see the sky.

Also, because it was fun to play "house" in there.

I wish Ben was here. He would kiss my forehead and tell me everything was going to be okay. Afterward, he'd take me home and make me some instant ramen — because he couldn't make chicken soup if his life depended on it. Then, we'd cuddle on the couch to watch *Futurama* until falling asleep.

Oddly enough, I didn't get my usual good morning text from Ben today. He must have been up late and decided to sleep in. But he knows today is my show. It's not like him to forget to wish me well before a big test.

As Professor Healy examines the photograph of our hideout from various angles, my phone begins vibrating in my back pocket — nonstop. One pulse of vibration after another, like a phone call that keeps ringing or when one of my Instagram pics goes viral and my notifications are blowing up. But I haven't posted any pics on social media in a few days. I've been too busy preparing for the show.

Bzzz. Bzzz. Bzzz. Bzzz. Bzzz.

Maybe my voicemail isn't working. Or maybe the mailbox is full. I'm notoriously guilty of letting unchecked voicemails pile up.

Bzzz. Bzzz. Bzzz. Bzzz. Bzzz.

The vibrating continues for what feels like at least five minutes straight, but is probably only a couple minutes. I finally pull the phone out of my pocket and apologize to Healy for the interruption. Glancing at the screen as I reach for the power button, I see a long list of Instagram mention notifications on my lock screen, and my heart drops along with my jaw.

2 min ago: @charleywinters have you seen this, girl?

2 min ago: lmao. @charleywinters just got dumped in front of 600K people. #sorrycharley

2 min ago: @charleywinters More like millions of people! This is gonna be news.

1 min ago: @charleywinters Don't pay attention to these assholes. You didn't deserve this. #sorrycharley

1 min ago: so fucked up. can't believe @officialbenhayes would do something like this to @charleywinters #sorrycharley

1 min ago: @charleywinters don't pretend you haven't seen this post. @officialbenhayes is too good for you. #byefelicia #sorrycharley #actuallynotsorry

1 min ago: haha! so true! Why doesn't @charleywinters get that bump on her nose fixed? #sorrycharley

"Charlotte, are you listening?"

I suddenly understood why Ben didn't text me this morning. I can literally feel my blood pressure dropping. My entire body feels cold and light as a feather, like I barely exist.

The room begins to spin as I look up from my phone screen. "What?" I murmur as Healy's red, bulbous nose comes in and out of focus.

I unlock the phone as my professor's voice murmurs in the background of my consciousness. Tapping the Instagram app, then a recent notification, I'm taken to a picture of Ben riding a motorcycle on the beach at sunset. Sitting on the back seat, with her head thrown back in gleeful laughter, is a blonde I recognize right away. A blonde the entire world could probably recognize.

The caption on the photo reads:

@officialbenhayes to new beginnings.
#instalove #newlove
MAY 11

I blink as Professor Healy steps around me so he's facing me straight on.

"I asked, 'How long is the exposure on this picture?'" he glances at the label beneath the frame then turns back to me. "The one titled 'Sky-house.' You've achieved a stunning depth of field with this lens. How long is the exposure? Based on the softness, I'm guessing it's at least a thirty-minute exposure, since it doesn't appear to be motion-blurred or out of focus or over-exposed."

I open my mouth to speak, but only one word comes out. "Exposed."

"Charlotte, your face is blood-red. Are you all right?" he says, grabbing my elbows.

I shake my head, still unable to speak as my phone continues to vibrate in my hand.

"Oh, dear. Let's sit you down. This is not the first time I've seen this happen," he says, placing a hand on the middle of my back to guide me toward a gold velvet tufted bench about ten feet away.

"Do you need some water?" the gallery curator, a middle-aged woman with dark hair as glossy as the marble floor, asks.

I shake my head again as I sit on the bench. "No," I whisper, reaching up to pull off my lucky scarf.

"Are you sure? Do you mind if I feel your forehead?" the woman asks gently.

I nod this time, closing my eyes and flinching slightly at the sensation of her cold hand on my face.

"Oh, my God. You're burning up. I'm calling an ambulance," she says, setting off to find a phone.

"Wait," I call out, holding up my still-vibrating iPhone. "I have a phone... Here. Take it. I don't want it."

As she walks toward me, I can't help but think about that chubby girl in my Spanish class. We are kin now. Today will be known as the day a single photograph changed my life.

The curator is a couple feet away from me when I lose my grip, dropping the phone on the floor as I pass out.

CHAPTER 1

CHARLEY

Now

Social media is a blessing and a curse. It can be used to galvanize support for important issues, like shedding light on social injustice. It's the best resource we have for sharing inspiring art and funny memes. On the other hand, social media has also become a means to pass judgment on people before they can defend themselves. The court of public opinion delivers its justice swiftly and without remorse.

I killed all my social media accounts about two and a half years ago. I'd rather be a nobody than a cog in that kind of machine. My friends, however, have started to question my commitment to this philosophy.

The yellow glow from the streetlight pours in through the glass storefront, illuminating Michelle's cinnamon skin as she hits the switch on the wall to dim the lights inside The Dunk seafood restaurant. Her silky black hair is pulled up tightly in one of those high ponytails that always make me wonder if she's secretly walking around all day with a massive headache.

Michelle works as the general manager at The Dunk, because her dad doesn't trust anyone else to run their family business. After locking the entry doors, she slides her jangling gaggle of keys into the front pocket of her black waist-apron and begins wiping down the tabletops.

I stand up from the table nearest the register, to stretch my arms and legs. Almost every Tuesday through Sunday, from eight p.m. to eleven p.m., I sit at this table to keep my best friend company while she closes up the restaurant. Sometimes, I help her clean so we can get out of there faster. Mostly, I use the time to edit photos on my laptop while chatting with Michelle.

"Is there any chili left?" I ask, closing the lid on my MacBook.

Michelle makes a mean chicken and white bean chili. Her mom, Monica, started making it for me when we were kids, when she realized I couldn't eat their original chili recipe because it contained pork sausage. It was one of the rare times my mother's

Jewish heritage resulted in the creation of a culinary masterpiece.

Michelle grabs a clean towel off the shelf under the counter and heads toward the dining area. "Julio! Pack me a quart of chili, please!" she shouts toward the kitchen.

"Okay, Mitch!" the cook shouts back.

"Want to hit the beach tomorrow?" I ask as I slide my laptop into the snug foam compartment of my waterproof travel case.

Michelle sprays lemon-scented cleaner on the table next to mine and nods. "Fuck yeah. I need a beach day," she replies, then sinks down into the seat across from me. "Which one?"

"Portuguese?" I reply, closing my laptop case and taking a seat again.

Michelle slides her phone out of the pocket of her blue skinny jeans, her top lip curling in disapproval. "Portuguese Beach is so crowded in the end of June."

"Not on Monday mornings. We can get there early to get a good spot, then book it when it starts getting too crowded in the afternoon."

She shrugs. "That's probably better. It's not like I need a tan."

Every time Michelle references her skin color, it makes me sad. It reminds me of the one time she let down her guard and admitted to me how she hated the way people treated her differently in the summer, when her cinnamon-brown skin became a rich coffee-brown. We all have things we hate about ourselves, physical features that feel more like betrayals than assets. For me, it's the bump in my nose I inherited from my Jewish mother. For Michelle, it's her skin color. For our other BFF, Allie Kim, it's her slanted eyes. Maybe that common thread of self-hatred is why we've been best friends since elementary school.

I pull my phone out of my pocket and text Michelle a single, lonely poop emoji.

She looks up from her phone screen. "If you need to release the chili demon, just go. You know you don't have to ask to use the restroom."

I smile as I let out a fart. "Not necessary when I can let it out right here. I just wanted you to look up from your phone."

She rolls her eyes as she understands this reference. "You have to dump him. Stat. That guy gives me the creeps."

The "him" Michelle is referring to is Tyler Bradford, the son of Mayor Tom Bradford, whom I started dating four months ago. Tyler has an annoying habit of texting me emojis to get me to look up from my phone when we're hanging out. Michelle and Allie do not like Tyler. To be fair, I don't know if I even like him. But in my opinion, being alone during the summer is worse than being alone during the holidays. If I do dump Tyler, it will be in September or October.

"He's not that bad," I say, opening up my bank account app to check my balance for the tenth time today, a new and disgusting habit I acquired recently.

Michelle looks up from her phone again and cocks an eyebrow. "The guy nicknamed you his 'little oyster.' He's a creep."

The smile on my face vanishes when I see my account balance. "Ugh. I need some new clients ASAP."

Michelle's face softens. "Are you in trouble? Like, are you not going to be able to pay your phone bill, or something?"

"It's not that bad…yet. But I definitely need to figure out a way to bring in more clients or it's R.I.P. Winters' Weddings."

She turns her attention back to her phone, types something, then turns the screen toward me. "Maybe if you put your photos on Instagram, like this girl, you'd get more business."

I stare at the Instagram profile for a girl named Elizabeth Messina, who Michelle follows on Instagram. "Yeah, and maybe if I hadn't failed my final exam, I'd have a degree I could use to get a job."

"You didn't fail your final. You refused to retake it," she replies as casually as if she were commenting on the weather.

"Really? This again?" I reply, my voice climbing an octave. "You're saying I was supposed to fight my way past the sweaty paparazzos so I could give a solo show of pictures depicting the places where my boyfriend and I had sex? The boyfriend who dumped me on Instagram?"

Her eyebrows shoot up as she looks up from the screen. "I'm just saying that maybe you could have chosen some different pictures and hired a bodyguard to get you past the paparazzi. If you really wanted the degree, that stuff shouldn't have stopped you."

I shake my head. "You know what happened the last time I tried to create another Instagram account."

I narrow my eyes at her, telepathically willing her to remember the time I created a new profile for Winters' Weddings. A client named "Isla" messaged me on Instagram and booked me to do her engagement shoot at a nearby vineyard in Sonoma. She even paid the fifty-percent deposit. When I got to the vineyard, I parked my car and entered the barn, where we planned to meet. "Isla" and her friends were there with their cell phone cameras at the ready to record my reaction to a cardboard cutout of Ben down on one knee proposing to Becca Kingsley, the pop singer he dumped me for. I vomited on the straw-covered floor and ran to my car.

I shake my head when Michelle doesn't acknowledge this catastrophe. "Forget it. I'm not arguing about this again."

"You're the one who brought up your cash flow

problems. I was just offering social media as a solution. A little self-promotion can't hurt, you know? And yet you still shoot me down, as usual. Anyway, we both know that's not what this is about."

"What are you talking about?"

She purses her lips. "I'm talking about that gigantic chip on your shoulder. It's been there since Hunter's graduation last month."

My eyes widen. "Are you kidding me right now? Are you accusing me of being jealous of my little brother?"

"There's a difference between bitterness and strength. You've gotten more bitter with every year that passes since you and Ben broke up. If you're not careful, you're going to push away the people who helped you get through that shit-storm. Which is sad, because we're the ones who actually love you."

I lower my gaze and take a deep breath to tame the angry lion inside me. I also try not to think about Ben, but the tattoo on my wrist makes that impossible. Michelle is pretty strongly implying that what Ben did to me indicated he was obviously not one of the people who *actually* loved me. But after three years, I still look at the tattoo on the inside of my left wrist and wonder if that's true. Could Ben have been pretending to love me for all those years?

I lay my hand over my wrist to cover the words "i love us" written in Ben's handwriting. He has a matching tattoo on the inside of his left wrist in my handwriting, if he hasn't attempted to get it covered up. During the four years that Ben and I were officially together, and the few years before when we hid our relationship from our families, we only got into one huge fight that almost tore us apart. Almost.

I remember vividly how I told Ben I loved him, but I didn't think I was secure enough to be with someone famous. He told me I had nothing to feel insecure about. "I don't like myself without you. Actually, sometimes I think you're the only thing I like about myself. I love you, Charley, and I'm not ashamed to say I love you more when you're mine. I love us." After that, "I love us" became our slogan. I cringe inside as I remember how we joked about trademarking the phrase.

"Let's change the subject," Michelle says, probably reading the signs in the painful expression on my face, the signs my mind has wandered into the dark corner where I hide my memories of Ben. "If you don't want to do social media — which I *totally* understand — then, maybe all you need to do is figure out what's worked in the past, you know, to generate business."

I lean my head back and sigh. "I feel like this is the hundredth time we've had this conversation. I don't know why you put up with me."

"Because I love you," she replied casually. "Okay, I remember when you were booking wedding shoots more than six months in advance because you were so busy. When was that? Two years ago? Maybe you were doing something back then that you might not be doing now."

I shook my head. "That was pretty much right after the breakup, when I first started the business. When people were still googling 'Charley Winters ugly cry' a thousand times a day. Bookings have steadily decreased since then."

Michelle winces at my reminder of the time a paparazzo published a video of me ugly-crying while talking to my mom in our backyard shortly after the breakup. The video went viral and, at its peak, the phrase "Charley Winters ugly cry" was Googled more than 800,000 times in one day. The video is still on every celebrity gossip channel on YouTube. I don't have the emotional fortitude or the money to hire a lawyer to force Google to take it down.

Michelle stands up and rounds the table so she can wrap her arms around my shoulders. "The only good thing I can say about Benjamin Hayes is that he's smart enough not to show his face around here anymore. I hope he gets antibiotic-resistant chlamydia and his dick falls off."

I laugh a little too hard and another tiny toot comes out. "I don't think that's how chlamydia works."

"I'm still holding out hope. And you really need to stop eating so much damn chili," she says, giving my shoulders one more squeeze before she sets off toward the back of the restaurant. As she rounds the counter, she glances back at me and flashes me a beaming smile, which quickly disappears as her eyes become fixated on something outside.

I glance over my shoulder toward the storefront and a flicker of intense pain fires through every nerve in my body when I see Ben standing on the other side of the glass.

To purchase Break,
please visit cassialeo.com/break

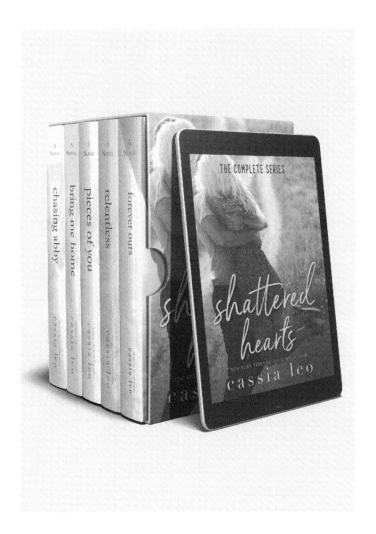

RELENTLESS ADDICTION

Mom is too tired to play hide-and-seek. Her stomach hurts so she took some medicine to make it feel better. I don't like it when she's sick. Grandma Patty doesn't know about Mom's stomachaches and I haven't seen Grandma in a few weeks, but I'm starting to think I should tell her.

Mom is asleep on the sofa; at least, I think she's asleep. I can't really tell the difference anymore. Sometimes, when I think she's sleeping, I'll try to sneak some cookies out of the cupboard. She usually hears me and yells at me to get out of the kitchen. Sometimes, she sleeps with her eyes half-open so I wave my hands in front of her eyes and make silly faces at her. She never wakes up and I always get bored after a couple of minutes. It's no fun teasing someone unless there's someone else around to laugh, and it's just Mom and me here.

Her skinny arm is stretched out over the edge of the sofa cushion and I stare at the bandage. It's too small to cover that big sore. One of those things she calls an abscess *opened last night while she was making me a grilled- cheese sandwich. Some thick, brown stuff oozed out of her arm. It reminded me of the glaze on maple donuts, but it didn't smell anything like a maple donut. The whole kitchen smelled like stinky feet when she put her arm under the water in the sink. Then she wrapped a billion paper towels around her arm and I had to eat a burnt sandwich.*

She didn't want to go to the doctor. She said that if she goes to the emergency room and shows them her arm the doctors might make her stay in the hospital for a long time. Then I'll have to live with people I don't know, people who might hurt me, until she gets better. My mom loves me a lot. She doesn't want anybody to hurt me the way she was hurt when she was nine.

Mom teaches me a lot. She isn't just my mom; she's my teacher. When she isn't sick, she teaches me math and spelling, but my favorite subject is science. I love learning about the planets the most. I want to be an astronomer when I grow up. Mom said that I can be anything I want to be if I just keep reading and learning. So that's what I do when she's sick. I read.

She's been asleep for a long time today. I've already read two chapters in my science book. Maybe I should try to wake her up. I'm hungry. I can make myself some cereal – I am *seven – but Mom promised she'd make me spaghetti today.*

I slide off the recliner and land on the mashed beige carpet that Mom always says is too dirty for me to sit on. I take two steps until I'm standing just a few inches away from her face. Her skin looks weird, sort of grayish-blue.

"Mom?" I whisper. "I'm hungry."

Something smells like a toilet and I wonder if it's the stinky abscess on her arm. I shake her shoulder a little and her head falls sideways. A glob of thick, white liquid spills from the corner of her mouth.

The memory dissolves as someone calls my name.

"Claire?"

The cash register comes into focus as the rich

aroma of espresso replaces the acrid stench in my memory. I've done it again. For the third time this week, I've spaced out while taking someone's order. The last two customers were understanding, but this guy in his *Tap Out* T-shirt and veins bulging out of his smooth bald head looks like he's ready to jump over the counter and either strangle me or get his own coffee.

"Sorry, about that. What was your order?"

"Wake the fuck up, blondie. I asked for an Americano with two Splendas. Jesus fucking Christ. There are people with serious jobs who need to get to work."

I take a deep breath, my fingers trembling, as I punch the order in on the touchscreen. "Will that be all?"

Baldy rolls his eyes at me. "And the scone. Come on, come on. I gotta get the fuck out of here."

"Hey, take it easy. She's just trying to take your order," says a voice. I don't look up, but I can hear it came from the back of the line of customers.

"I already gave her my order three fucking times," Baldy barks over his shoulder. "Mind your own fucking business."

Linda comes up from behind me, placing a comforting hand on my shoulder as she sets the guy's Americano on the counter next to the bag holding his multigrain scone. She doesn't say anything, but the nasty look she casts in his direction could make an ultimate fighting champion piss his pants. Linda is the best boss in the world and one of the many reasons I still work at *Beachcombers Café*. All the other reasons I still work at one of the tiniest cafés in Wrightsville Beach have to do mostly with my desire to disappear after dropping out of UNC Chapel Hill ten months ago. But that's a whole other story.

Baldy peels the lid off his coffee, rolling his eyes as he peers into the cup. "I said I wanted room for cream. Are you all fucking retarded?"

Before I could reach for the cup, a guy in a suit steps out of line, grabs the cup off the counter, and dumps the entire contents into Baldy's scone bag. A loud collective gasp echoes through the café.

"Now you've got plenty of room for cream," the guy says.

I clap my hand over my mouth to stifle a laugh as Linda scrambles to get some paper towels.

The rage in Baldy's eyes is terrifying. "You motherfucker!" he roars as my hero grins.

And what a sexy hero he is. Even in his pressed shirt and slacks, he can't be more than twenty-two. He has an easygoing vibe about him, as if he'd rather be surfing than wearing a suit at seven in the morning. With his sun-kissed brown hair and the devious gleam in his green eyes, he reminds me of Leonardo DiCaprio in one of my favorite movies, *Titanic*.

Baldy charges my Jack Dawson, but Jack swiftly steps aside at the last moment. Baldy trips spectacularly over a waist-high display of mugs and coffee beans. All six people in the café are now standing silent as Baldy spits curses at the cracked mugs and spilled beans underneath him.

I look at my hero and he's smiling at me, a sneaky half-smile, and I know what he's about to do.

Before Baldy can get to his feet, Jack drops a few hundred-dollar bills on the counter. "For the damages."

He winks at me as he steps on Baldy's back then hurries toward the exit with no coffee, just a huge grin that makes everybody laugh and cheer. He gives us a quick bow, showing his appreciation to the crowd, and slips through the door as Baldy lumbers to his feet.

My gaze follows Jack as he slides into his truck, one of the newer models that looks like something conceived in the wet dreams of a roughneck and a *Star Wars* geek. He pulls out of the parking lot and disappears down Lumina Avenue.

I have a strong urge to whisper, "I'll never let go, Jack," but I'm pretty good at keeping my urges to mutter lines from *Titanic* to myself; especially when there's a six-foot-two 'roided-out freak staring me down. Something snaps inside me as I remember what started this whole fiasco.

I step aside so Linda can take over and I skitter

away through the swinging door into the stockroom. I unfold a metal chair and sit down next to a small desk where Linda does the scheduling. Pulling my legs up, I sit cross-legged on the chair, place my hands on my knees, and close my eyes. I take a long, deep breath, focusing on nothing but the oxygen as it enters my lungs. I let the breath out slowly. A few more deep breaths and the whole incident in the café never happened.

Some people are addicted to heroin. Others are addicted to coffee. I'm addicted to meditation. No, not medication. Meditation.

Meditation doesn't just relax me; it helps me forget. It's like a friend you can count on to say just the right thing at the right time when that thing you want them to say is nothing. Meditation is the friend who intervenes when you're about to say or do something very stupid. Like three months ago, when meditation saved me from taking my own life after I realized I had become my mother.

RELENTLESS MEMORIES

I haven't been to a party with my best friend Yesenia Navarro in ten months. The last time was the Halloween bash at Joey Nassau's house where I got stuck talking to Joey's thirty-something cousin who spent three hours attempting to convince me to go back to school. I want to go to tonight's party at Annabelle Mezza's house about as much as I want to eat a spoonful of cinnamon. Tonight's party will be packed with all the people I have been successfully avoiding for ten months.

"I'll be velcroed to your side the whole night," Senia assures me as I gather my purse and a bottle of water from the kitchen counter.

Senia thinks I'm a freak because I never leave the apartment without at least one bottle of water. I've spent enough time avoiding the various other substances my mother abused. She could hardly call an addiction to water and meditating a bad thing. This doesn't stop her from trying. And true to best-friend form, every day when she comes home from work she still brings me a six-pack of my drug of choice. To say that I love living with my best friend would be a huge understatement.

"Whatever," I mutter. "It's just down the street. I'll walk home if things get too uncomfortable."

"Speaking of uncomfortable." Senia cocks an eyebrow as she examines my outfit: faded skinny jeans, a plain white tank top, a green hoodie that's three sizes too big, and a five-year-old pair of black Converse. "Is that what you're wearing?"

Senia could be a supermodel with her perfectly

tanned skin, dark tousled hair, and spot-on fashion sense. At five-ten, she towers over my five-foot-six frame in her four-inch heels. She has the perfect button nose and full lips that I've always dreamed of having. My blonde hair is too thin, my nose is too small, and my upper lip is too big. Senia says it gives me a sexy pout, but she only says that to make me feel better. I'm average and I've learned to not only accept it, I embrace it.

"Don't make me say it," I reply as I unscrew the cap on the bottle of water and take a swig.

She holds up her hand to stop me. "Please don't. And, by the way, that has to be the *worst* motto ever adopted by any person ever in the history of all mankind."

I pull my keys out of my purse to lock the front door as we make our way out of the apartment. "You might be exaggerating just a little bit."

Her heels click against the pavement and I inhale a huge breath of briny ocean breeze as we walk to the covered parking spot where Senia keeps her new black Ford Focus. She isn't rolling in cash, but her parents make pretty good money with the real-estate company where their entire family works. She works in one of their satellite offices in Wilmington while the rest of the family works at the main office in Raleigh. Her parents pay her half of the rent on our apartment, her entire UNC tuition, and she gets a new car every two years on her birthday. Nothing fancy, but new.

"I get it," Senia says as she deactivates her car alarm and we slide into our seats. "You don't want to be a shallow, vacuous piece of shit like Joanie Tipton. But that doesn't mean that you have to dress for a party like you're going to work on a fucking construction site."

"Hey, I resent that. I left my tool belt at home this time," I tease her and she rolls her eyes as she turns on the stereo to her favorite EDM station.

An Ellie Goulding dance mix blasts through the speakers and Senia immediately begins bobbing her head as she pulls the car out of the parking space. She maneuvers her car around the moving truck that's half-blocking the exit out of the complex. Cora, our eighty-six-year-old landlord, must have finally found a tenant for the upstairs apartment.

"Claire!" Senia shouts as she pulls onto Lumina. "You need to renew your driver's license!"

"Senia! I live four hundred feet from where I work and I don't have a car. I don't need a driver's license just so I can be your designated driver."

I sold my car when I moved to Wrightsville Beach two and a half months ago to pay for the first and last month's rent on my apartment. Senia moved in three weeks later, once the semester ended. She claimed she did it so we could spend the summer together on the hottest surf beach on the East Coast, but I know it's so she can help me with the rent for a few months. The summer is halfway over now and she'll be moving back in with her parents in a month to go back to UNC. If I don't find another roommate or convince Linda to give me more hours at the café, I may be homeless in six months – for the third time in my life.

As soon as Senia pulls up in front of Annabelle's parents' beach house, I smell the beer and hear the laughter. My chest tightens. I focus my eyes on the water bottle in my hand, forcing myself to think of nothing else as I breathe deeply and slowly. Senia is quiet as she waits for me. She's used to my coping mechanisms.

The edges of my vision blur and everything but the bottle disappears. I think about how water is the essential element for life to flourish. I think of how it soothes and carries us, cleanses and quenches us. I imagine the water washing away every worry, every doubt about tonight and carrying it away to a clear, tranquil sea. I close my eyes and take one final deep breath as my muscles go slack and I'm completely relaxed.

I nod once and reach for the door handle. "Okay. Let's do this."

"I don't know how you do that, but it's kind of creepy and inspiring all at once."

Senia and I stroll up the walkway arm-in-arm past

the lush summer garden toward the blue, two-story clapboard beach house. I spot a group of five guys standing on the porch with red Solo cups and cigarettes clutched in their hands. From his profile, I recognize the short Indian guy leaning against the porch railing. He was in the sophomore Comp Lit class I dropped out of last October. I turn my head slightly as Senia and I climb the steps to the front door, hoping none of them will recognize me.

Senia pulls open the squeaky screen door and I choke on the sweet smell of alcohol and perfume. We step further inside and the first thing I see is a gathering of a dozen or so people huddled around the sofa where a guy with a guitar is playing and singing a Jason Mraz song.

This memory is too strong to fight.

I walk through the tall door into my ninth and final foster home. As luck would have it, the woman I called Grandma Patty eight years ago was actually just our closest neighbor. I had no family to take me in after my mother died. I'm only fifteen, but I'm already more jaded and cynical than my forty-something caseworker. She flat out told me that this would be my last placement. If I screw this one up, I'll be sent to a halfway house until I turn sixteen in four months. The moment I step into the living room, I know I'll be seeing the inside of that halfway house soon.

Three guys sit around a coffee table, two of them on the sofa and one cross-legged on the floor with a guitar in his lap.

The one with the guitar wears a gray beanie and his dark hair falls around his face in jagged wisps. He's humming a tune I recognize as a Beatles song my mom used to play whenever she cleaned the house: "I Want You."

The thud of my backpack hitting the floor gets his attention and he looks straight into my eyes. "Are you Claire?" he asks. His voice is smooth with just a touch of a rasp.

I nod and he immediately sets his guitar down on the floor in front of him. My body tenses as he walks toward me – as my "training" kicks in. The reason I've been in and out of foster homes for the past eight years since my mom OD'd is because of everything she taught me.

From as far back as I can remember, my mother taught me never to trust men or boys. She was so honest and candid with me about the things her uncle did to her from the time she was nine until she was fourteen. She told me all the things to look out for, all the promises these predators would make. The most important thing to remember, she told me, was to never let them think you were a victim because that was when they pounced.

I followed my mom's advice for eight years and I hadn't been so much as hugged the wrong way. I'd kept myself safe, but only by getting myself kicked out of every foster home at the slightest hint that someone might see me as prey. This guy in the beanie doesn't look like a predator, but looks can be deceiving.

He grabs the handle of my backpack and nods toward the stairs. "I'm Chris. I'll take you to your room."

Senia shakes my arm and the living room comes back into focus. "Are you okay?"

I nod quickly and she gives me a tight smile. She knows what just happened, but she's willing to shrug it off because she knows that's exactly what I need tonight. No long talks about getting over the past or seeing a shrink. People have endured far worse than I have. There's devastating famine and wars being waged across the globe. I have nothing to complain about – except the fact that I really don't want to be here tonight.

I spend the entire night hiding my face every time someone I recognize enters the room or explaining how I dropped out because I couldn't pay my student loans. No one here knows the truth. The one smart thing I did last year was drop out before word could spread around campus.

At twenty minutes past midnight, Joanie Tipton finally enters the living room and casts a lazy smile in my direction, and *now* it's time to leave. Joanie is the only person here, besides Senia, who knows why I dropped out. I had to beg Joanie, on my knees, not to tell anybody. It was the second most humiliating moment of my life.

I grab Senia's arm and whisper into her ear, "Don't

look now. Mr. Jones just arrived. I have to get out of here."

Mr. Jones is the nickname Senia gave Joanie after she got a chin implant the summer before our sophomore year and we decided she now looks like a transvestite version of Bridget Jones. She even has Renee Zellweger's scrunched eyes. It would be funnier if she didn't hold my secret in her French-manicured hands.

"I'll take you home," she whispers back and I shake my head adamantly.

"No! I'm just going to sleep. You don't need to come home for that. I'll walk."

Her eyebrows furrow and she nods. "Breaking all the rules tonight, huh?" She's referring to the fact that I never walk the streets alone at night. "I know you're sleeping in so I guess I'll see you when I get back on Monday. Love you."

I kiss the top of her head as I rise from the sofa and scoot past her. I glare at Joanie from across the room as I leave, though she isn't looking at me. She's already engaged in a flirtation with a guy who's at least ten years older than us. God, I wish I had a secret on her.

I duck out of the house and pretend to adjust my bangs as I pass a couple making out next to a car in the driveway. The last thing I need is to be recognized as I'm leaving. As soon as I'm out of the couple's line of sight, I pick up my pace. Our apartment is only two and a half blocks away. The only reason Senia drove here is because of her monstrous heels.

I rush out into the crosswalk, eager to get away from the party – and the memories. I don't see the headlights until it's too late.

Visit cassialeo.com/shattered-hearts to continue reading Shattered Hearts, an epic rock star romance spanning 25 years.

ALSO BY CASSIA LEO

CONTEMPORARY ROMANCE

Stand-alones
Raise Your Game
Temperance
Break
Her Guardian
Knox
Black Box
Luke
Chase

Shoot for the Heart Series
Dirt (Book 1)
Seed (Book 2)
Bloom (Book 3)

The Story of Us Series
The Way We Fall (Book #1)
The Way We Break (Book #2)
The Way We Rise (Book #3)

To Portland, With Love (Book #3.5)

Shattered Hearts Series
Forever Ours (Book #1)
Relentless (Book #2)
Pieces of You (Book #3)
Bring Me Home (Book #4)
Abandon (Book #5)
Chasing Abby (Book #6)
Ripped (Book #7)

ROMANTIC SUSPENSE

Stand-Alones
King
Knox

Unmasked Series
Unmasked: Volume 1
Unmasked: Volume 2
Unmasked: Volume 3

For more information, please visit
cassialeo.com/books

ABOUT THE AUTHOR

New York Times bestselling author Cassia Leo loves her coffee, chocolate, and margaritas with salt. When she's not writing, she spends way too much time re-watching *Game of Thrones*. When she's not binge watching, she's usually enjoying the Oregon rain with a cup of coffee and a book.

Send Cassia some love at:
cassialeo.com/contact
contact@cassialeo.com

Made in the USA
Middletown, DE
23 September 2020

20442136R00170